Then she reached up and pulled out the pins so her hair cascaded downwards.

She heard him sigh, softly.

'Like that you're beautiful, Erin,' he said.

'Come and sit by me. You said you used to want to stroke my hair—well, now you can. Feel just above my left temple.'

So he did. His face was close to hers; it had to be. His touch was gentle, but still she jerked a little when he got close. 'Two scars and signs of stitches.'

'The first scar was the result of an accident. The second was an operation to relieve pressure inside the skull.'

She saw the understanding dawn on his face. 'The fall off the cliff,' he said. 'With David King on Striding Edge. When you got engaged.'

The GPs, the nurses, the community, the location…

LAKESIDE PRACTICE

a dramatic place to fall in love...

Welcome to **Keldale**, a village nestled in the
hills of the beautiful Lake District…where the
medical staff face everything from dramatic
mountain rescues to delivering babies—
as well as the emotional rollercoasters of their own lives!

Also in the *Lakeside Practice* trilogy:

THE DOCTOR'S ADOPTION WISH
THE MIDWIFE'S BABY WISH

THE DOCTOR'S ENGAGEMENT WISH

BY
GILL SANDERSON

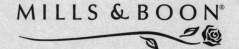

MILLS & BOON®

All the characters in this book have no existence outside the imagination of the author, and have no relation whatsoever to anyone bearing the same name or names. They are not even distantly inspired by any individual known or unknown to the author, and all the incidents are pure invention.

*First published in Great Britain 2003
Harlequin Mills & Boon Limited,
Eton House, 18-24 Paradise Road, Richmond, Surrey TW9 1SR*

© Gill Sanderson 2003

ISBN 0 263 83456 5

*Set in Times Roman 10½ on 12 pt.
03-0703-50562*

*Printed and bound in Spain
by Litografía Rosés, S.A., Barcelona*

CHAPTER ONE

ERIN didn't really know why she was coming back.

It had been a long journey from London, and it had rained all the way. Now, as the train rumbled on the last few miles to Windermere, it was raining even harder than ever.

They pulled up at the last little stop before her destination. Someone opened the door to step out of the carriage and Erin caught a smell she remembered. The raw, evocative smell of the damp countryside. She shivered. It was so much colder here than in London.

For the first eighteen years of her life she had lived near here, and after she had gone to London to study medicine she had spent every holiday here. Until two years ago. Since then her visits had been as brief as possible. And even her parents had moved down to the south coast.

Coming home was supposed to be exciting, comforting. She didn't feel either excited or comforted.

She shivered again. It was not her way to back out of a fight and she knew she was going to have to fight. She'd have to meet him…some time. But then she'd go back to practising medicine in London and she'd be the Erin she had been two years before.

Time to think of something more cheerful, and perhaps inevitably she thought of Jeremy. Dr Jeremy Barley. Erin smiled quietly to herself. They had just met—as friends, that was. Previously they had been doctor and patient.

She had had a fair number of boyfriends—but not for a while. It was good to have someone as a friend and nothing more. Jeremy was a supportive colleague, he didn't want to be her lover.

It was Jeremy who had suggested that she take a year away. 'You still don't know how you feel,' he had said. 'Your body might be cured but your mind is still fragile.'

'The last thing I am now is fragile,' she had told him. And this was true—partly.

It was September now and the nights were drawing in. Through the train window the fells appeared nothing but a dark line against the slightly lighter sky. The odd solitary light made the view seem even lonelier. Her flat in London looked across a sea of lights at night, towards Alexandra Palace in the daytime. It was a view she now much preferred.

But she was quite looking forward to her new job. For a year she was to be a GP registrar at Keldale, being trained by Dr Cal Mitchell. She had liked and admired Cal when he had interviewed her. She felt that she would learn from him. And a spell in the country would be good for her. After this she would spend all her life in London.

The train was slowing now, they would soon be in Windermere. She stood, reaching for her overnight bag. Her other luggage had been sent up the week before. Rain rattled against the carriage window. Time to start her new life.

Cal was waiting for her on the platform, a tall, tough-looking figure whose very appearance seemed to generate confidence. 'Typical Lake District weather.' He grinned at her. 'Welcome to the practice, Erin.'

'I remember the weather and I can cope with it. I've

brought my boots and anorak. It's good of you to come to meet me, Cal.'

'It's nothing, we're going to work together. And everyone in the practice helps everyone else.'

He leaned over, took her bag from her. 'Your main luggage arrived yesterday, it's in your cottage already. Now, let's get moving before it starts to pour again.'

Quickly they ran to where his Range Rover was parked by the side of the station. For a short while there were streetlights shining on the wet road surface, but soon enough they were in the complete darkness of the countryside, with only the headlights for illumination. She pulled her coat round her. It didn't get as dark as this anywhere in London.

'I hope you'll be happy working at the practice,' Cal said. 'Technically I'm to be your trainer but I hope you'll learn from everyone.'

'I'm looking forward to it. In hospital everyone seemed to be in a hurry, I often didn't like to ask questions in case I held people up.'

Cal laughed. 'We're always in a hurry, too. But if there isn't enough time to help someone new then I'm not doing my job right.'

'I'm sure you are.' She thought for a minute, then asked as casually as she could, 'In your last letter you said there'd be another registrar working at the practice.'

'Yes, we've got another trainee, he's been with us for three months. Doing very well, he'll make a fine GP. In fact, he's another local, he remembers you from school. He's called Josh Harrison, a year older than you but he's been out in Africa for a year. Remember him?'

In the dark, Erin frowned. Josh Harrison? Yes, she remembered him.

'He was a year ahead of me, I think. A good rugby

player, did a lot of walking and climbing.' Memories of her schooldays, not entirely happy, came flooding back. 'He was big but he was…quiet. Lovely curly hair.'

Cal laughed again. 'He's still big, still playing rugby and climbing, and he gets more results by not asking questions than many doctors do by asking too many. You'll work well together. You didn't see much of him at school, then?'

'Not an awful lot. I tended to run with a different crowd. In those days I was very interested in acting and the amateur dramatics lot tended to hang together.' She paused and then went on, 'I was a different person then.'

'Possibly. Now, there's a turning here…we go up this track.' The Range Rover started to bump and lurch its way upwards.

'This isn't the way to Keldale,' Erin said.

'We're going to Leatherslack Farm. Since I'm in the area I thought I'd call on Mary Benson. She came out of hospital after abdominal surgery a couple of days ago and I want to check up on her. But you're still wearing your town shoes so you can stay in the car if you like. They'll only get filthy in the yard.'

'My shoes will clean. I'd like to come with you if I may.'

He smiled. 'You'll be very welcome. Mary likes visitors.'

He pulled up in the farmyard and they were invited straight into the kitchen by Billy Benson, Mary's husband. 'Glad you called, Dr Mitchell,' he said. 'We were going to phone the nurse tomorrow morning. Mary's been in a bit of pain—more than before.'

'Let's have a look, then.'

They were shown into Mary's bedroom. Mary, a tough-looking fifty-year-old, tried to smile at them.

'Sorry to cause you trouble, Doctor,' she said. 'I suppose I ought to expect to hurt after I've had a hole cut in me.'

'It's no trouble and I don't like seeing my patients in pain. Billy said it's got worse.'

Mary shrugged. 'Who knows what to expect?'

Cal asked if Mary minded Erin being there, and if she could conduct the examination. Mary was entirely happy. 'We all have to learn, love,' she said to Erin. 'If I can help, I'll be happy to.'

So Erin examined Mary's abdomen. She was as gentle as she could be as she eased back the dressing, but she guessed from the hissing of Mary's breath that she had still caused her pain.

A normal surgical scar. No, not normal. The wound was angry. There was erythema, a reddening round the site. It had swollen and there was some pus exuding. Carefully, Erin took a swab and slid it into a phial. Then she asked, 'You didn't feel something give in the wound—perhaps when you were exerting yourself? No sudden increase in pain?'

'No. I've looked after myself, or Billy has. And the pain came on slowly.'

Next Erin palpated the sides of the wound, being as gentle as possible. Then she looked at Cal. 'What's your diagnosis?' he asked.

'I think the wound is infected. We'll send the swab to be cultured, to make sure. There's cellulitis round the wound so there's infection in the subcutaneous tissue— I suspect streptococcus. I don't think the muscle layers have split. I suggest treatment with penicillin or erythromycin.'

'I agree entirely. And I have the penicillin in my car. What d'you think of Dr Hunter, Mary?'

'She's got soft hands. She'll be good.'

* * *

They were dropping down into Keldale village now. Erin remembered it—she had visited it in the past, though she used to live on the other side of Kendal. They splashed past an attractive-looking pub called the Red Lion and after five minutes pulled up outside a row of four tiny cottages. They belonged to the practice, and one of them was to be hers while she worked there.

Cal didn't get out of the car at once. Instead, he looked at the end cottage, and in the light of the dashboard Erin could see a smile on his lips.

'My fiancée Jane lived in that cottage for a few weeks,' he said. 'In that cottage we really got to know each other. Happy times, Erin. I hope you'll be as happy living there.'

'I'm lucky to have somewhere so nice,' she said. 'I did have a quick look round and I know I'm going to be comfortable here.'

It had started to rain again now so he took her case and they ran to the front door. He unlocked it, turned on the hall light and they stepped inside. Then his mobile rang.

She had noticed that he kept it fitted to the car dashboard, but when he left the car he carefully unhooked it and put it into his pocket.

'Cal Mitchell here.'

She watched as he listened, his face becoming more and more grave. Then he said, 'Of course I'll come round, Alice. About twenty minutes. But you do know there'll be nothing I can do? No, it's no trouble at all.'

The call ended and he looked seriously at Erin. 'I'm going to have to leave you to find your own way around. That was Alice Brent. She's been nursing her husband at home for the past five months. He's got an inoperable brain tumour and it looks as if his time has come. She's been expecting it but…she'd like me to be there.'

'Shall I come with you?'

He shook his head. 'This isn't medicine, Erin, it's friendship. But thanks for the offer. I'm sorry I can't show you where things are but I—'

'I'll help Erin get settled.'

Erin jumped. Where had that voice come from? It was a soft but a deep voice. She turned, and just outside the door was a figure, haloed in the rain. A large male figure.

'Thanks, Josh, that'd be a great help,' Cal said. 'Erin, welcome to the practice again. I'll see you tomorrow morning. Get in about nine. Jane says when you get settled that you must come round and meet Helen again. Now Josh will look after you and I'd better go.' He thrust the phone into his pocket, ran for the Range Rover. A moment later it roared away.

For a moment Erin stared silently at the figure outside. Then she said, 'You'd better come in.' He followed her as she walked a couple of steps and found the switch for the living-room lights. Then they looked at each other and Erin nearly swayed with the shock.

She remembered Josh Harrison as a schoolboy, neat in his uniform. Even though he had been big, he had been shy, had had little to say. He hadn't been a member of the in crowd that she had belonged to. But over the past ten years he had changed.

It wasn't his appearance—though he had lost the expression of schoolboy innocence that she vaguely remembered. His face was calmly friendly, his hair still had the dark curls that so many of her friends had envied, now enhanced by drops of silver rain. She had recognised him at once—which was odd, since they had never been more than acquaintances.

But as they stared silently at each other there flashed some kind of message—a different kind of recognition. Josh was now a man and she was aware of his maleness, of what he could mean to her. Already he was inspiring feelings in her that made her uneasy. And something told her that he felt exactly the same way.

She shook herself irritably. This was silly. All it was was a recognition that Josh had grown into quite a handsome man. She had met many handsome men, her last hospital had been full of them. It was just that she was tired, imagining things, non-scientific things like instant attraction. And the last thing she needed now was any kind of intense relationship. That could only harm her.

But she could feel something pulsing between them, and knew he did, too.

'Hello, Juliet,' he said, after what seemed like an eternity. Still that soft deep voice.

But he had said the wrong thing. He had annoyed her, though he wasn't to know why. 'My name is Erin—Erin Hunter,' she snapped. 'Nice to meet you again, Josh.'

Feeling oddly formal, she held out her hand to him. He took it in both of his, held it in a way that was almost a caress. She liked it, but after a while she took her hand back.

He smiled. 'I'm afraid you'll always be Juliet to me. I sat at the back for every rehearsal of the play, watched it for the three nights it was on. I thought you were wonderful in the part. It almost made me want to change from biology to English.'

To be honest, she knew he was right. She had acted as she had never acted before or since. But that was a long time ago, and it was now clouded with unhappy memories. Sharply, she said, 'That was nearly ten years ago. I'm a doctor now, not a schoolgirl in a school play.

And the only reason you were there every night was because you'd been roped in to shift scenery.'

He didn't seem to notice her annoyed tone. 'Not exactly,' he said. 'I could have played cards with the other scene shifters. But I chose to watch you—you and… Wasn't it David King playing Romeo? You were good together.'

How could he upset her so much? She guessed that he was merely being polite, trying to make her feel at home. And this was what she had come back here to face. But she couldn't stop her voice sounding sharp.

'That was a long time ago. I don't want to reminisce, I want to look forward. As I said, we're doctors now, not schoolchildren.'

'True.' He had now recognised her annoyance, but seemed more curious than put out himself. 'I hope we'll be good neighbours,' he said. 'And since we're registrars together, we'll be seeing a lot of each other.' He considered this a moment, and then his voice became more practical. 'Now, shall I give you a five-minute tour of the premises and then leave you alone to unpack? You see there's a fire lit here and your luggage has been taken upstairs.'

It did only take five minutes to look round the little house, to see where the meters were, how to operate the central heating system, what to do when the back gutter overflowed. Then he said, 'I've got some studying to do now. But I've done a large pan of spaghetti Bolognese— it's my student signature dish. If you want to come round for a quick meal in an hour or so, you'd be very welcome. Nothing fancy, this isn't a formal dinner invitation.'

Erin was hungry, but he had upset her, both by the shock of his appearance and by his references to her acting and David King. So she lied. 'I ate on the train, but thanks anyway. I think I'd better unpack, get things straight and have an early night.'

He appeared unfazed by her rejection. 'As you wish. But if you change your mind, or if you have any queries, just knock.' He turned just as he was about to leave. 'Oh, and welcome to the practice from me, Erin.' There was a blast of cool air as he opened the door and then he was gone.

She decided that the best thing to do was to work. First she had another quick look round the cottage, and she loved it. It was decorated and equipped with unobtrusive good taste. Then she changed into jeans and shirt and made the bed—a double, she noticed. Oh, well. She quickly unpacked, stacking her clothes in the built-in bedroom units, lining up her books and files in the bookshelves downstairs. She cleaned the shoes she had dirtied in the farmyard.

In the kitchen she found a box with tea, coffee, fresh milk and bread and enough food for an evening meal and breakfast. There was a note from Jane, Cal's fiancée. 'A few groceries to start you on your new life. Hope you'll be happy with us. Looking forward to meeting you again. Love, Jane.'

Erin was touched. She had met Jane, who was both Cal's fiancée and the district nurse, when she had come up for interview. She had liked her—and the little girl Helen. No one had ever welcomed her like this in any other new place. Perhaps she could be happy here. And then, after half an hour, she realised she was hungry.

She could make herself a quick meal. Or she could walk down to the Red Lion in the village—she remembered that they served good meals and bar snacks. But she had come back here to regain some of her lost confidence. And she would have to work with Josh in the future. Perhaps it would be a good idea to go to see him, to talk about their training together.

Then she remembered that flash of instant attraction—and put it to the back of her mind. It had been nothing. The surprise of meeting again after so many years. She could ignore it. She would have to ignore it.

Before she could change her mind again, she hurried outside and knocked at the cottage next door.

'I didn't mean to be ungracious,' she babbled when Josh appeared, 'but I really would like to come to supper if I may?'

He was as calm as he had been earlier. 'You're very welcome. Will you come in now?'

'No, I can see you're working. In about half an hour?'

'That'll be great. Settling in all right?'

'I'm doing fine. Half an hour, then.' And she was gone.

She went back to her own cottage, found things to do and then did things whether they needed doing or not.

'I haven't got a bottle of wine to bring,' she said when he opened the door for her.

He waved her inside. 'It doesn't matter. I've got a bottle of supermarket offer-of-the-week red. In fact, I've got a caseful, there was five per cent off for bulk orders.'

'I hope I'm not living next door to a secret drinker!'

'Nothing secret about it. A glass of wine improves any dinner. Shall we have one before we eat?'

She showed her into his living room. The shape of the room, the furniture were both very similar to her own living room. But there was the definite impression of Josh's personality. There was a throw on the couch in barbaric but attractive reds and blacks.

He saw her looking at it. 'It's a Navaho blanket. I bought it last year when I was climbing in New Mexico.'

'It's lovely. And how did I guess that you were a climber?'

There could be no doubt about that. The only pictures on the walls were of mountains or rockfaces. There was one of Josh in full climbing kit, waving cheerfully at the camera. And, far below him, in sickening detail, Erin could see a valley floor. She recognised the scene at once. Josh had been climbing on El Capitan, in Yosemite valley. He must be good. How could he do it?

'Climbing keeps me sane,' he said. 'No matter how hard I've been working, half a day on a rockface and I'm refreshed.'

He poured her a glass of wine and handed it to her. 'Don't I remember that you used to do some climbing?'

She shrugged. 'Just a bit of walking. But I've left that all behind me now. I wouldn't worry if I never saw another mountain. I'm here for a year and then I'll probably spend the rest of my life in London.'

'Never want to see another mountain? That's a terrible thing to say!' He looked at her curiously. 'Is there any special reason for it?'

He was astute! She turned away to hide her confusion, peered into the kitchen.

'No reason at all. As I grew up I…just lost interest. What's that wonderful smell? Is it garlic?'

He seized on her hint. 'Dinner shall be served at once, ma'am. In fact, we'll eat in the kitchen if you don't mind.'

He led her through, seated her and refilled her glass. 'This isn't haute cuisine. But it's nourishing and filling.'

'And it smells so good it must taste all right. Shall I help myself?'

He placed two dishes on the table, one of spaghetti, one of a rich red sauce. There was also a block of Parmesan and a grater. She noticed that the Bolognese sauce was obviously home-made, he hadn't just opened a jar. And it did smell good. Then he opened the oven and took out two garlic bread rolls. They smelt even better!

'You can't eat this meal and be graceful,' he said with a grin. 'You're bound to spill something. Here, have a napkin so you don't spoil your shirt.'

It was a wonderful meal. She hadn't realised how hungry she was, and both dishes were empty by the time they had finished. Then they had fruit and coffee, and she felt at peace with the world.

Erin realised she'd never really known Josh while they had been at school. He had a quiet, mischievous sense of humour, a sardonic way of looking at life. They talked about people they vaguely remembered, old friends who had drifted away.

'We're unusual,' he said after a while. 'D'you realise, nearly three-quarters of the people we've mentioned are married now? And most of them have at least one child.'

She shrugged. 'That's medicine for you. It's not only a career—it's a lifestyle. And when you start you just don't have time for that kind of full-time commitment.'

'I'm glad you agree with me. So I take it you're not in any kind of, well, permanent relationship now?'

'Why do you ask?' Her voice was sharp again.

Josh shared the last few drops of wine between them. Casually, he said, 'We're going to be working together. It's the kind of thing you get to know about your workmates.'

She thought about this, then said, 'I've no great need

for any kind of relationship. I'm just not interested. And I have my career to think of.'

It sounded a clumsy explanation even to herself, but it was true and it was all she was willing to give.

He looked at her thoughtfully. 'At school people thought that you and David King were an item. Everyone thought you'd get married in time.'

'Everyone was wrong! I never had any intention of marrying David! I had my medical career to look forward to. I wanted to be a doctor and that was all I was interested in. David was a friend and that was all.' Then a thought struck her. 'You haven't heard anything about him and me, have you? Anything recently?'

'Not a thing. Why, is there anything to hear?'

'I just don't want to talk about my schooldays. They're over and...'

She reached for her wine and in her anger tried to drink it while still speaking. A mistake. She coughed, choked and spluttered into her napkin. He stood to pat her on the back and then fetched her a glass of water. After a couple of heaving breaths she felt better.

'Listen to me,' she said, her voice still strangled. 'The last of the great sophisticates. Can't even drink a mouthful of wine.'

'It could happen to anyone. You were saying about your schooldays?'

'They're over, long over, Josh. I want to look forward now.'

'A good idea. I'll get you a coffee then we can sit in the living room.' He grinned. 'At school all we could talk about was leaving, how we were going to have interesting and eventful careers afterwards. Well, we've had them. And what do we talk about after ten years? School again.'

'Quite. And now we're grown-up. We're reasonable human beings, we've joined the vast majority of the reasonable human race.'

'If you think the human race is reasonable,' he said darkly, 'you're going to get a nasty shock when you start as a GP.'

'True. D'you like working here, Josh?'

'I love it,' he said simply. 'I even like it when people do daft things. That's what makes them people. They have feelings, ideas that they can't quite understand. Illogical, non-scientific ideas.'

She thought he was trying to tell her something, she wasn't sure what. 'Give me an example,' she said.

He grinned again. 'At school you were the Golden Girl.'

He remembered that! She had almost forgotten it herself. 'Just a silly nickname.' She shrugged. 'Because I had fair hair. Now give me this example of illogical thinking.'

She realised that in spite of his careless manner he was watching her quite closely. He said, 'Well, before, when I saw you for the first time since we were at school together, I felt a sort of…well, the attraction we all felt for the Golden Girl suddenly came back. It was as if you were seventeen and I was eighteen again. Quite a strong feeling, really. But I suppose it was just the shock of seeing you again.'

'I felt something, too,' Erin said. 'But, like you say, it was just the shock of seeing someone again.'

She looked at him, conscious that she had crossed a tiny bridge and was not sure where it would lead. They had both admitted to the attraction. Calling it the shock of seeing someone again was just an excuse.

He went on, 'I'm sure that's all it was. Well, we'll

have to see.' She saw him make a conscious effort to relax as he went on, 'I've been here three months and I've learned more from Cal than—' There was a knock at the door.

He looked at his watch and frowned. 'Perhaps that's Cal calling back, but I thought he... I'll go to see.'

She heard the mumble of voices at the door, and then a stone-faced Josh ushered a woman into the room. 'Erin, this is Annabelle Prentice. Annabelle works for Cawston's, that new pharmaceutical company that set up near Kendal.'

Erin stood and offered her hand. She was conscious that she was dressed casually, in shirt and jeans. Annabelle, on the other hand, was dressed in an obviously expensive grey suit, with jewellery, shoes and accessories to match. Somehow she seemed to have dodged the rain that was still pattering outside. Her face was expertly made up, unsmiling and beautiful. She touched Erin's hand, dropped it at once.

'Annabelle's called to pick up a couple of books I borrowed,' Josh said.

'They'll be in the bedroom,' Annabelle said coldly. 'That's where I left them.'

'Quite. Would you like a coffee?' Josh spoke reluctantly.

For the first time Annabelle smiled, a small, toothy smile. 'No, thank you. I'm meeting my managing director for a late supper meeting in half an hour. There are things we have to discuss.'

'Of course. I'll fetch the books, then. Do sit down, Annabelle.'

Annabelle sank gracefully into the nearest chair and Erin sat, too.

'I gather you're another trainee like Josh,' Annabelle said, obviously not really caring.

'We're called GP registrars now. We are qualified doctors.'

'Yes, quite. I thought of training for medicine myself, but…' Annabelle shrugged, to show that she hadn't been tempted for long.

'These are the books you wanted,' Josh said, suddenly appearing in the room, 'I found a couple more you didn't mention.'

Annabelle rose, accepted the books. 'You can keep these two if you want,' she said, inspecting them. 'They might be useful to you. I'll be off to America in a week, the office will buy me American editions.'

'No, you have them,' Josh said. 'I really would prefer that.'

'Very well.' Annabelle looked at Erin. 'Nice to have met you,' she said insincerely. 'Do keep an eye on Josh for me, won't you? But he doesn't waste much time for a heart-broken man, does he?'

Erin saw the muscles tighten in Josh's jaw, but he didn't say anything. Annabelle looked round, smiled briefly. 'I wonder how long I'll remember this room?' she asked of no one in particular, and then Josh followed her as she made for the door.

Nothing was said for a while when Josh returned. He sat opposite her, his eyes and his thoughts obviously far away. Tactfully Erin yawned and then stood. 'I'd better be going myself,' she said. 'I've had a long day and I'm quite tired.'

'But it's still quite early,' Josh said half-heartedly.

'I'll go anyway. Thanks for the meal, Josh. I did enjoy it. And it's been an…interesting evening.'

'Hasn't it just,' Josh said, and managed a grim smile.

*   *   *

In fact, Erin did go to bed quite early. But she didn't sleep at once, there were things she needed to think about. She sat there, holding her cocoa, hearing the rain rattling on the windows. She felt warm, protected.

First the good things. She knew she was going to be happy in this cottage and she thought that she'd work well with Cal and learn from him. She wanted to be a good GP.

Now Josh, her new neighbour. She liked him. Partly, of course, because of how he remembered her—as the Golden Girl. Any girl would be pleased to be remembered that way. And there had been that sudden flash of—flash of what? It had been so strong! She wriggled irritably, as if she was suddenly uncomfortable. She was a doctor, she didn't believe in instant attractions. She was just tired, that was all. Besides, the last thing she needed now was a relationship.

But he was rather nice.

And Annabelle? What was the relationship between him and Annabelle? When they had been together the atmosphere had crackled with hostility.

Erin put down her cup and switched off the light. And for the first time she thought about her real reason for coming to Keldale. The biggest problem was yet to be faced. Well, she would settle in for a week or two—and then she would see to it. She would lay her ghosts if she could.

She wondered about the nightmare. It had been a while since she'd had it, but she was back here now and…she would have to see.

CHAPTER TWO

'I KNOW you've gained some experience,' Cal said. 'I know you've had eighteen months of post-graduate training. But I want you to go through the same induction that everyone else in the practice does. It's important that you learn to work as a team member, and that means having some idea of what everyone does. The practice nurse, the midwife, the receptionists, the practice manager, the pharmacist, everyone—they are all important. Then there's the people in the district that you need to know.'

He handed Erin a folder. 'I wrote this myself. It will tell you all about our conditions of service, the area, our work and how we try to do it.'

She leafed through the folder. It was impressive. 'I like the idea of an induction,' she said. 'I've been thrown in at the deep end so many times, been told to get on with it and pick up what I can. This is so much better.'

Cal grinned. 'It's good to hear that,' he said. 'I believe that if you know what you're doing, then you'll do it well. You can't learn by trial and error if you're dealing with patients.'

It was the following morning. As requested, she had arrived at nine o'clock, feeling slightly apprehensive. But Cal had been there to greet her and it was obvious that he took his duties as a trainer very seriously. He was going to spend much of the morning with her.

'Later on you can spend an hour with Eunice, the practice manager,' he said. 'She'll go through your contract with you, get you to sign various things. She's also arranged the lease of a four-wheel-drive car for you—you can pick up the keys from her. You need a tough car round here.'

'You seem to have thought of everything,' Erin said, slightly overwhelmed.

'I try to. It's my job.' He led her through into a store-room. On a table were three large bags.

'Doctor's bags,' he said, pointing to them. 'You'll carry all three in the boot of your car. A lot of your time you'll be visiting people who live some distance from the nearest chemist—from the nearest neighbour, in fact. You need to be equipped and have medicines for almost any emergency.'

She moved to the table, looked down at what was there. In hospital, where she had spent most of her time so far, there had always been all the instruments, all the medicines, all the instruments and facilities she could possibly need, right to hand. There had been expert professional advice if she hadn't been sure what she was doing.

'Quite often I'll be working on my own now, won't I?' she asked. 'It's a bit frightening.'

'You're never on your own. We're a team, we work as a team. Whenever you make a visit or set of visits out of the surgery, then you leave word where you are going. And you keep your mobile phone handy at all times. We all need to keep in touch.'

'That makes sense. I'll remember.'

He opened the first bag. Erin peered inside. He said, 'This is the usual doctor's bag. It contains all the diagnostic equipment you're likely to need. There's nothing there that you're not used to.'

She peered at stethoscope, a packet of disposable

gloves, tendon hammer, syringes—all the usual tools of her trade neatly displayed. 'I've used all of those at some time,' she said.

'Good.' He smiled sardonically. 'And you'll notice that this other half of the bag is packed with forms. Everything from a prescription pad to a Mental Health Act form. Remember, it can be tedious, but always keep your paperwork up to date. Otherwise you'll end up in chaos.'

He opened the second bag and she saw rows of drugs, neatly labelled and packed in foam. 'Our pharmacist makes this up and replenishes it when things run out. Like I said, a lot of our patients live a fair distance from the nearest dispensing chemist.'

It was a full bag. She saw analgesics of various strengths, antibiotics, antihistamines, drugs for the respiratory system, gastrointestinal problems. There were diuretics, insulin, treatments for poisoning and accidental overdoses.

'This seems to cover everything,' she said.

'Remember, if you're in a farmhouse miles from anywhere, and there's a foot of snow outside, you need to have things handy.'

'I see.' Erin opened the last bag herself, saw a portable defibrillator, airways, the large needles needed for an emergency tracheostomy.

'Emergency resuscitation equipment,' Cal said briefly. 'I hope you won't have to use any of it. But you have to be prepared. Just in case.'

'And do I carry all of this every time I make a call?'

Cal grinned. 'Just the first bag. The rest stays in the car. You can usually guess what drugs you might need and take them out of the second bag.'

'I'm impressed,' she said honestly.

Cal snapped shut the bags. 'You won't be going out

by yourself for a couple of weeks but they're here, waiting for you. Now, I thought you might like to spend the rest of the morning observing in the antenatal clinic and this afternoon you can go out with the midwife on her rounds and see a bit of the countryside.' He grinned, and just for a moment Erin recognised how attractive he was. 'You'll like Lyn Pierce. You know that some time soon she's going to marry Adam, my partner?'

'Everybody knows,' Erin said with a smile.

'He'll just have to wait until I've married Jane. We decided first.'

'I've met Lyn briefly,' Erin said. 'I think Adam is a very lucky man. And I've met Jane, and you're lucky, too.'

Erin enjoyed her morning session. She had attended antenatal clinics before in the hospital, but this one was run slightly differently. For a start, Lyn was pregnant herself. 'I thought I was a good midwife,' she told Erin when the two of them had a moment together. 'I thought I knew it all. But you've got to experience it to know what it's like.'

Proudly she stroked her bump. 'Put your hand here,' she said. 'You can feel her or him kick.'

Erin did as she was told. 'Yes, I can feel a kick,' she said. 'A healthy one, too.'

Lyn smiled serenely. 'That's a doctor talking,' she said, 'which is fine. But one day you'll feel that kick yourself and you'll realise that you only ever knew the half of things.'

For a moment Erin was envious. It must be marvellous to be so certain of your future, to know that you loved, and were loved by, a wonderful man. Was this something that she would ever feel?

Lyn stood and smiled. 'Work calls,' she said. 'One thing is certain. There'll always be babies.'

There was more time to chat to individual mums, more gossip about local affairs. Erin noticed that Lyn introduced her each time and mentioned that she was a local girl. And Erin then was instantly part of the accepted team.

'This is like a family, not a surgery,' she said when she and Lyn were having a quick cup of coffee. 'Everyone knows everyone else.'

'Cal always says that we treat people, not illnesses,' Lyn said, 'and I think he's right.'

Erin thought of her own vast hospital in London. Many people she saw once and never again. The hospital was efficient—but in many ways it had to be impersonal. 'I like it here,' she said. 'I like treating people.'

She had a full but enjoyable morning. Then at lunchtime, as she sat in the doctors' lounge eating a sandwich, Josh came and sat with her.

She couldn't quite understand her feelings. She was pleased to see him—after last night he was now a known and friendly face. But she did feel just a bit too pleased when he sat near her? He was certainly a good-looking man.

She shook herself irritably. New job nerves, that was all.

'Did you have a good first morning?' he asked, grabbing a sandwich from the tray on the table.

'I had a frightening first morning. I'm a qualified doctor now, I'm supposed to know things. I've just learned how little I do know.'

Josh laughed. 'That's supposed to be the first step towards wisdom. But you'll learn a lot here. Cal's a great trainer and everyone else will pitch in to help you.'

He ate his sandwich and said nothing as a couple of the other staff came in, greeted them then retired to the other end of the lounge. Then, in a slightly lowered voice, he said, 'The end of last night was a bit embarrassing. For you and for me. I'd like to make it up to you, try to give a slightly better impression.'

'What had you in mind?' she asked cautiously.

'We could go down to the Red Lion tonight for an hour or so. There'll be other people there who know us, it's almost like the practice club. And you might even meet a couple of people you were at school with. Shall I call for you about nine o'clock?'

She thought for a moment. There were several good reasons why she shouldn't go out—she was tired, she had preparation for tomorrow, there was some studying to do. But... 'All right,' she said. 'I'd love to come.' She found she was rather looking forward to it. Just as one friend with another, of course.

Erin knew what she'd wear in London if she was invited out for a drink—probably to a wine bar. She'd wear a smart dress, or perhaps a pair of black linen trousers with a silk top. But here she found herself putting on jeans and a sweater, digging out a pair of sensible shoes and deciding which waterproof coat to wear. And probably in London she'd take a taxi. Things were different here. She'd walk. She rather liked the change.

Josh knocked at exactly nine o'clock. It wasn't exactly raining, but there was a fine drizzle, and he held a large black-and-white umbrella. She was pleased to see he was dressed exactly as she was.

At first he walked by her side, holding the umbrella over her and carefully keeping his distance. So she said, 'You'll get wet,' and moved closer to him. His hip brushed hers and occasionally their arms touched. She didn't mind.

'This is my doctor's umbrella,' he said as they paced together. 'It's a good stout one. I'm often asked to be the doctor for my rugby club and I stand under it on the touchline.'

She laughed. 'You don't still play, then?'

'I certainly do. But they have to decide whether they want me as a doctor or a winger. We like to have a doctor standing by on match days.'

'Can't you be both?'

'I have been. I was playing when a woman fainted in the crowd. I was called off the pitch, and the referee didn't know whether to allow it or not. And the woman woke up to find a big wet muddy man stooping over her. She screamed with the shock.'

Erin giggled. 'What was wrong with her?'

'Well, at first I thought nothing very much. You know, these things happen. I was just going to recommend that she have a cup of sweet tea and then go home but then I noticed that she had a low pulse and there was very small volume. So I persuaded her to go to hospital for a check-up. In fact, I insisted. It took some doing, especially since I'd just started training and I was a bit unsure myself. And she obviously thought that wet, muddy doctors weren't as competent as those with suits and stethoscopes. But she went to hospital, and it turned out that she had Stokes-Adams syndrome. Her fainting was the result of cardiac failure. Later she had surgery for aortic stenosis.'

Erin was curious. 'So how did you feel?'

'Still wet, muddy and getting rather cold.'

She prodded him in the ribs. 'Not then, you idiot!

After you found out that she was really, seriously ill and you had detected it.'

'Well,' he said, 'I felt rather proud of myself.'

They walked on for a while, then she said, 'If I'd asked that question of any of my London friends, they'd have given me some smart-aleck answer. But you were honest.'

'Honesty can be a two-edged sword for a doctor. But at the moment we're friends, not doctors. Now, there's the pub ahead.'

She liked the Red Lion. The walls were panelled and there was no music. Josh found them a smoke-free room. From the dining room there escaped the most delicious smells and she decided that some time soon she'd come here for a meal.

Josh smiled and nodded at a dozen people, then fetched her a glass of red wine and a beer for himself.

For a while they talked about her day, what she had learned, how she was going to enjoy herself here. Then she said, 'You're avoiding coming to the point, aren't you? We're here to talk about…about last night.'

He laughed ruefully. 'You'll be a good doctor. A few minutes' general chat with the patient is fine. But quite soon you want to know symptoms so you can proceed to a diagnosis.'

'And then treatment and cure?'

He laughed again, but this time there wasn't much humour in it. 'There are some things that medicine can't deal with,' he said.

Josh didn't say anything more for a while and she decided to give him time to think, to work out what he wanted to say. She could see his eyes flicking across the room, looking from person to person as if seeking inspiration.

He had a striking face, she thought. Not convention-ally handsome, but a face you looked at twice. And the more you looked at it, the more you liked it. But it was the face of a man you wouldn't want to cross. There was determination there, an almost ruthless determination to do what was right.

'I enjoyed your company last night,' he said eventu-ally. 'And I think we got a few things sorted out. We both recognised that there had been that…that…'

'It was purely physical,' Erin said. 'A moment's mu-tual attraction. It must have happened to you a dozen times before.'

'It has. But never as strongly as it did last night,' he said bluntly.

She was put out by this but she tried not to show it. It wasn't what she wanted to hear because she, too, had felt the strength of that instant appeal. It was more than she could ever remember having experienced.

'Just a hangover from your schooldays,' she dis-missed. 'We're both older, wiser, more experienced now. We can deal with this kind of thing.'

'I hope we can deal with it. And a hangover from schooldays, possibly.'

He looked at her thoughtfully. 'Erin, I had a lecturer in Sheffield who said that it was wrong to turn to science for an answer for everything. Sometimes you have to rely on your heart, not your head.'

She knew that her own heart was beating slightly faster. 'You mean we should pay some attention to that…to that…'

'Just recognise it,' he said. 'Perhaps even accept it.'

They were sitting in a busy room with groups at all the tables around them.

But suddenly the hum of conversation seemed far

away, other people faded into near invisibility. There were only the two of them in their own tiny world. And she wasn't ready for it, she had to escape. 'Tell me about Annabelle,' she said.

He looked at her, and his little smile told her that he knew exactly what she was doing.

'You think she was making a point, coming back for those books?' he asked.

'Those books in your bedroom. Yes, I'm certain of it.'

He was going to go along with her deliberate change of subject. He took a deep draught of his beer and then said, 'I've known Annabelle for about a year. We met when I was working in the hospital in Sheffield. She worked for a pharmaceutical company, there was a party and after that we saw a lot of each other. Then I got the position here—and after a while she found a job in Cawston Pharmaceuticals, about twenty miles away.' He laughed, not very convincingly. 'I thought she got the job to be close to me. The fact that it was promotion was irrelevant.'

'She's entitled to her career,' Erin said.

'I agree. Both our careers were important. I was willing to fit in with her plans, to make adjustments if necessary. Anyway, we talked of getting married, I thought it was settled. Then Annabelle was offered a further big promotion in America. I hope I'm doing her an injustice, but I think it was because she'd got quite…close to the American managing director.'

'And you had no part in her future plans?' Erin guessed.

'Exactly. We had a massive row, I told her what I thought of her.'

He grinned, this time rather sheepishly. 'Probably not

a good idea, whatever the situation was before the row. Afterwards it was completely beyond repair. I'm afraid I was rather angry.'

'She didn't seem too pleased to see you yesterday,' Erin said. 'So what now?'

He shrugged. 'I like women, I really do. But I suspect it'll be quite a while before I…before I…'

'Let someone else break your heart?' Erin guessed.

'Something like that.' He held up his empty glass. 'Emotion makes me thirsty. What about you going to the bar and getting us each another drink?'

'Done,' she said. As she walked to the bar she realised that asking for another drink had been a ploy on his part to gain some time to calm himself. And when she returned he was in a totally different mood.

'So it's goodbye, Annabelle, hello, Erin,' he said cheerfully.

'I'm not replacing Annabelle, that's certain. But the pair of us ought to get on as friends. I've had my share of emotional problems and they drag you down.'

He looked at her curiously. 'Problems? What sort of emotional problems? Are you going to tell me what dragged you down?'

'No,' she said. 'Well, not yet. You haven't…you haven't heard anything about me, have you?'

He looked at her curiously. 'Nothing at all. Should I have?'

'No, I was just being silly. Anyway, that's enough emotion for one night.' Erin took a quick mouthful of wine. 'Didn't you live on a farm when you were at school?'

He looked at her speculatively then decided to go along with this new abrupt change of subject. 'I did indeed. My parents were tenant farmers, and after I went to medical school they got a better farm down south.'

He grinned again, and she thought how happy he looked when he did. 'But now my dad's got a new job as farm manager on a big place just the other side of Kendal. He's so happy to get back here, and I'm happy to be here, too.'

She was trying to remember him at school, trying to recall what they might have said to each other. But it was hard. All she could remember was that curly hair.

It was strange, how comfortable she felt with him. They were talking like old friends, jumping from subject to subject, at times quite happy just to sit and be silent. She hadn't felt this comfortable with a man in years.

'You're a quieter girl than I remember, ' he said after a while. 'At school you were a star, the centre of everything you did. Like I said, the Golden Girl.'

What he said was true, she had to admit it. She shrugged. 'People change,' she said. 'When you're seventeen, eighteen…you think the world is going to be a lot simpler than it turns out to be.'

'True. Is that why you changed? Because of life's complications?'

Once again she realised he was more shrewd than he appeared. He would find out about her in time—or perhaps she would tell him. But not yet. She liked their relationship as it was at present. Then she blinked. Relationship? She had barely known him for twenty-four hours.

At that moment a couple came over to their table. Josh introduced them as a local businessman and his wife, and they sat down. Shortly after that they were joined by a man on his own.

'It's a friendly pub,' Josh whispered to her.

She decided she liked it. She was enjoying herself. And they didn't have chance of any further intimate conversation.

They only stayed an hour and then they went back to their side-by-side cottages. The rain had stopped and they walked easily together, talking about work and what she was expecting to learn.

'I left my bedroom light on,' she said, looking upwards.

'So you did.' He stood for a moment, looking upwards, then said, 'I'll only say this once. ''What light through yonder window breaks? It is the east, and Juliet is the sun.'''

'I told you before, I'm not Juliet! My name's Erin. Nine years ago I had a part in a school play. Since then I've moved on. I'm not Juliet and I certainly don't want a Romeo. It's a stupid play anyway. You can tell from the start that those two characters are going to get things messed up.'

'I liked the play,' he said, unperturbed. 'But I won't quote it again if you don't like it.'

Erin sighed. 'Sorry. I guess I overreacted. I've enjoyed the evening, Josh. We'll do it again some time.'

'I'll look forward to it,' he told her. Then he kissed her on the cheek and went into his cottage.

The rest of the week was hard work—but fun. Erin spent some time observing Cal, some time with the other members of the practice, then had a morning seeing her own patients, this time with Cal as the observer. She enjoyed it.

On Friday morning Cal called her and Josh in and said, 'I want you to go out together. Visit Mr and Mrs Templar, they live at 29 Fell View. They're both getting on a bit and at the moment Jane, as district nurse, is calling in once a week, giving Mr Templar his injections for arthritis.'

He pushed two thick folders across the desk. 'Here are their case notes—have a look before you go.'

'Are we calling for any specific reason?' Erin asked.

Cal shrugged. 'They both like a call from the doctor. Just give them a quick looking at, make them feel that they're important, that people care about them.'

'We'll go through the notes first,' Josh suggested when they got out of Cal's room. 'Then we'll take my car. What did you think of Cal's suggestion that this was little more than a social call?'

'Rubbish,' Erin said cheerfully. 'This is some kind of test.'

Carefully they read through the notes, writing down anything that appeared important. Elsie Templar was eighty-two, Brian Templar eighty-five. They both appeared to be in reasonable health, though Brian suffered from arthritis and couldn't move very far and Elsie had broken her hip a couple of years previously and had never quite regained her confidence. She could walk but again not very far. Otherwise, they seemed fine.

'Cal says if you don't know, then ask,' Erin said. 'I saw Jane come into the surgery earlier on, I'm going to ask her what she thinks of Brian and Elsie. She sees them once a week. Cal didn't say we weren't to ask, did he?'

'I'm sure he'd approve. Let's go and have a word together.'

'Elsie and Brian? Both bright as a button,' Jane reported. She grinned, as if she guessed that Cal had set them a test. 'Certainly no sign of mental degeneration. Both retired teachers. They read the daily paper, watch the news and comment on it, get books delivered by the local library every week. They keep that cottage spotless, and somehow manage to keep the garden tidy, too. They'll enjoy a visit.'

'So let's go and see,' Josh muttered.

The cottage was on the outskirts of the village, the last in the row. Opposite it there was a wall and then the steep slope of the fell, leading upwards to a wooded crest. Josh had to park round the bend, some distance away, so as not to block the road. And, as predicted, they were made very welcome.

After the introductions, the necessary chat and a cup of tea each—made by Brian—Erin examined Elsie and Josh examined Brian. And when they met again in the living room, Erin looked at Josh, who shook his head. She shook hers, too. Neither of them had found anything.

'You both seem to be in good shape,' Josh said. 'Apart from a bit of trouble getting about, everything seems to be fine.'

'Keep the brain going and the body will follow,' Brian said.

'You were reading me an article about it yesterday, weren't you, dear?' Elsie said. 'Now, where is that paper?'

She bent to peer at the shelf under the coffee-table.

'Is this it here?' Erin asked. 'It's right under your nose, Elsie and…'

And then she understood.

'Could I, please, have a look at your eyes, Elsie?' she asked gently.

'Not necessary,' Elsie said, speaking crossly for the first time. 'I can see perfectly well with my reading glasses and my long-distance glasses and I—'

Brian's voice was sad but firm. 'Elsie, dear, you can't go on pretending any longer. Dr Hunter has spotted what's wrong. Let her look in your eyes.'

So Erin looked in Elsie's eyes with the ophthalmoscope and saw the cataract at once. Josh came to look and check.

'We'll arrange a visit to a consultant,' Erin said. 'I'm pretty sure it's only a cataract, but we need to be sure and there is treatment available. Why didn't you mention this before?'

'I thought it was just one of those things that happened when you got old,' Elsie said defensively. 'And Brian's been reading to me.'

'We'll see if you can read yourself,' Erin promised, taking the form from the bag. 'Now we'll see if we can get you in as quickly as possible. And one of us will call again some time next week.'

'That'll be nice,' Brian said.

'You spotted that and I didn't,' Josh said as they walked away from the cottage. 'I'm impressed, I really am.'

'I was examining her, not you. I should have noticed it before.'

'She was trying to hide it from us. Strange, how some old people—'

In the distance they heard the soft thud that meant that reinforced glass was being broken. They turned the bend in the road and there was Josh's car—and a youth looking through the broken back window. He heard them coming, turned and ran, something clutched in his hands. 'Hey!' Josh shouted, and ran after him.

But the youth had a start. He dropped what he had been carrying. Quickly he climbed the wall beside the car and as he dropped behind it they heard a yell of pain.

Then they saw him again, limping but still moving quickly up the fell. Soon he was lost in the woods.

Josh started to climb the wall but Erin put her hand on his arm to stop him. 'Leave it,' she said. 'We're doctors, not police or social workers. We'll just go and report it.'

Josh walked back to the car, picked up what the youth had dropped. A small plastic bag containing a few tools for the car. 'Not really worth getting hurt for, is it?' he asked. Then he looked over the wall where the youth had climbed and fallen. He winced, and pointed to something. 'I suspect he fell on that old barbed wire. He could have hurt himself quite badly. And it's clearly a doctor's car—perhaps he was after drugs or something. We've got to find him, Erin.'

'How?'

'He's in the woods, watching us right now. But he can't stay up there all day. We get into the car, drive away. There's a path that runs along the top edge of those woods that leads down into the village. In half an hour he'll come walking down it. Then we'll nab him.'

'You're supposed to be Dr Watson, not Sherlock Holmes.'

'Remember what Cal said—we try to treat people, not illnesses. That lad needs treatment.'

'I'm still not convinced it's our job. But if you want…'

In fact, it was surprisingly easy to catch the boy. They parked just round the corner from where the path came into the village. After twenty minutes a doleful-looking lad limped down the path and Josh grabbed him and marched him to the car.

'Get into the back seat,' Josh said. 'First of all we'll

have a look at the cut on your head and the scratches on your knee. Are your tetanus jabs up to date?'

The lad looked unbelievingly from Erin to Josh. 'Think so,' he muttered after a while.

'Well, keep still while I look at what you've done to yourself.' There was silence for a couple of minutes as Josh dressed the cuts on head and leg. Then he said, 'Now, what's your name and address? Don't try anything clever or we'll have you straight round to the police station.'

There was a pause before he replied. 'Peter Marsden. I live at—'

'We're going to check. So tell the truth.'

The words came out with a rush. 'I live at 20 Sykes Road. Please, don't tell my dad, it'd kill him. And my mum, too. I'll get you the money for the window, I swear I will. It's just that he said that…well, he said that a doctor's car would have…'

'What are you on, Peter? What are you taking?'

'Just a bit of weed every now and again. And ecstasy when I go out with my mates.'

'And who told you to thieve from a doctor's car?'

It took some doing, but all the fight had left Peter. Eventually he told them the name of the older boy at school who had supplied him with drugs, who had offered him a free supply if he found anything worth stealing in a doctor's car. 'What are you going to do now?'

Josh's voice was gentle. 'I'm going to give you a chance, Peter. I want you to come round to the surgery tomorrow with your father. For a start, I want to check those cuts on your head and leg. Then I think we might be able to arrange some treatment for you and there'll be no need to contact the police.'

'But my dad will—'

'He's entitled to be angry. But you might find he's more sympathetic than you know. Now, I'm going to drive you home. After that it's up to you.'

'That was all my decision,' Josh said after they'd dropped Peter off and were heading back to the surgery. 'If I'm wrong then I'm responsible.'

Erin thought for a minute, then said, 'No. It was *our* decision. If I'd wanted, I could have objected, insisted that we call the police. But I didn't. Just one thing. The minute we get back we tell Cal. We tell him everything.'

'You bet we do,' Josh said, with considerable feeling.

First they told Cal about their visit to Brian and Elsie Templar, about how Erin had found the cataract in Elsie's eye. 'Did you know about the cataract?' she asked. 'Was it some kind of test?'

'Just something a good doctor should detect,' Cal said smoothly. 'Did you find anything else?'

'I'm afraid we did,' Josh said.

Cal listened to their story without comment. Then he said, 'I'm impressed. You've taken a big risk but I think did the right thing. You've given a young lad a chance—let's hope he deserves it. Anyway, if things go wrong, I'm going to back you up all the way.'

'Even though we took a risk?' Erin asked.

Cal smiled. 'You'd be surprised how many risks doctors have to take,' he said.

CHAPTER THREE

THAT afternoon Erin was working in the practice library, looking up case histories of illnesses suffered by farm-workers who had been exposed to pesticides. Cal had said it would be of interest to her as they had the odd case. She was enjoying herself, it having been weeks since she had studied like this. There was something compulsive about chasing a reference from book to book, trying to understand exactly what a problem was and how it could be dealt with.

Then the library door behind her opened. Somehow she knew who it was, and she felt the hairs on the back of her neck tingle with—anticipation?

Josh stood behind her for a moment, then placed a hand on her shoulder. She shivered and felt an urge to reach for the hand, to press it closer to her.

This was foolish! She just didn't want this kind of feeling. She jerked back in her chair, looked over her shoulder at Josh and said mildly, 'You're disturbing me.'

'How I wish I could,' he said. 'But work calls. Cal asked if the pair of us could go for a word with him.'

'Not the headmaster's study again,' Erin muttered. 'I feel like the bad girl of the fourth year.'

When they went in Cal's room they found he had two visitors. One was Peter Marsden, looking, if possible, even more hangdog than ever. The other was an older, tougher-looking man, by his features obviously Peter's father. With a shock Erin saw that he was wearing a clerical collar.

'Drs Hunter and Harrison,' Cal said formally. 'The two people who helped your son this morning. Erin and Josh, this is the Reverend Marsden.'

The man bounced to his feet, shook their hands. 'I have to thank you both for the compassion and understanding you showed my son,' he said. 'I know you didn't take the easy way. Now, first of all, he has something to say to you.'

A greatly embarrassed Peter then stood and muttered an apology and promised to pay for the broken car window. His father looked on reflectively.

'I think we can put the broken window behind us for a while,' Cal said. 'The question is what do we do with Peter. Would you be willing to go for drugs counselling, Peter?'

Peter indicated that, yes, he would.

'There is a further problem,' Josh now broke in. 'Apparently Peter gets his drugs from school. It's a situation we can't really ignore. We have to do something, or tell someone. There are other young people at risk.'

Erin saw the Reverend Marsden looking approvingly at Josh. 'In fact,' he said, 'I am one of the governors of the school. If you here are all willing, I will happily take on the responsibility of telling the headmaster and making sure that something is done. And, I assure you, it will be.'

Cal looked at Erin and Josh. 'These are the doctors concerned,' he said. 'What to do is their decision.'

Josh glanced at Erin, who nodded back. Josh said, 'I think that's an ideal solution.'

'Good,' said the Reverend Marsden. He took out a cheque-book. 'Now, I must insist on paying for the broken window.'

'I'd rather Peter paid for it,' Josh said.

His father looked at the boy. 'He will pay,' he said, in a gentle but steadfast voice. 'He must learn that we all have to pay for our mistakes.'

'I think you'd better take Peter next door and have a closer look at his injuries,' Cal said to Josh. 'And thank you both for coming down.' The meeting was obviously over.

Erin went back to the practice library but she couldn't concentrate on what had been fascinating not fifteen minutes before. And after a while Josh came in again, and sat on the other side of the mahogany table. They were alone together.

'A good afternoon's work?' he asked. 'I came to see if you agreed with everything we decided.'

'I was there,' she pointed out. 'I was quite capable of saying if I disagreed. In fact, I think it an ideal solution—if there is a solution.'

'I see. It's just that at the end I thought you looked at me as if you disapproved. I wanted you to agree with me, Erin.'

'I do agree! It wasn't the decision, it was...' She found that she didn't want to say any more, but now she had started, she would have to. 'It was you. You're a pusher. If you think something is right, then you'll fight for it, no matter what the cost. You felt sorry for Peter but were determined he should pay—for his own good.'

'Is that a fault?' he asked quietly.

She shook her head. 'No, it's a virtue. But sometimes it's hard to live with.' She wondered if she could live with it. Possibly not.

A week later there was something new to try.

Erin felt apprehensive. She had seen video recordings of herself before, but only when she had been acting, pretending to be someone else. This was going to be different. She and Josh had been recorded interviewing a patient.

'Remember, these videos have been made with the permission of the patients concerned,' Cal said. 'They are a teaching aid, a chance to see yourselves as others see you.' He grinned at the couple sitting with him. 'And if you think you look and sound terrible—don't worry. Everyone feels the same.' He slipped the first video into the recorder.

Erin glanced at Josh, but he seemed calm enough. Well, he'd been through this experience before.

It seemed strange, seeing him on a television screen. There was the consulting room, and Josh sitting by his desk, speaking to an older man. After a preliminary examination, Josh asked the man to bend, to stretch, to try to touch his toes, to move from side to side. Erin thought he was doing everything perfectly correctly. Then the man sat again and Josh went behind his desk.

'This is where it gets…problematic,' Cal said.

'I'm sorry,' Josh was saying, 'but I can't issue you with another sick note. Your back problems were only mild to start with, and you've been cleared by the consultant at the hospital. You've had a long time off work. Quite frankly, Mr Summers, there's no reason why you shouldn't go back to work tomorrow.'

'There is a reason,' the man said, his voice now growing angry. 'My wife's ill, you know that. She just can't cope with the three kids on her own. I've got to be there to help her!'

'I'm sorry and I sympathise. Perhaps you can work something out with Social Services, I can give you a number. But the fact remains, you are fit to work.'

The man's voice became cajoling. 'Why go to all that

bother? Just sign me off for another month. Other doctors would do it.'

'Possibly other doctors would. I won't. You can say what you like, but I refuse to lie for you.'

'Well, thanks very much! I'll go where I get a bit of understanding!'

The man stormed out of the surgery and slammed the door behind him. Josh remained still in his chair, his face showing no emotion whatsoever. Then the screen filled with dancing white dots.

'Well,' Cal said. 'Now you've seen the replay, would you have handled things any differently? Incidentally, let me say that no GP ever satisfies all of his patients. You're going to get angry ones. You're going to have to put up with insults and possibly even injury at some time in your career. It goes with the job. Josh?'

'I think my examination was OK,' Josh said slowly. 'I think my diagnosis was correct and my decision was right, too. It was how I told the patient.'

'Good. Your fault was?'

'I wasn't sympathetic enough.'

'Nearly. What do you think Erin?'

She didn't like criticising Josh, but she knew it was for his own good and that he wouldn't hold it against her. 'One sentence,' she said. 'In fact, one word really. "I refuse to lie for you." In effect you called him a liar and then suggested that you were…you were better than him.'

'Ouch,' said Josh. 'Is that how I came across, Cal?'

'It wasn't the most diplomatic thing to say,' Cal said, being diplomatic himself. 'Now, let's play that scene again, I'll be the patient and see if you can be more…gentle with me.'

It was an interesting exercise and Erin started to realise that there was a lot she had to learn—not about medicine but how to apply it to people.

Then it was her turn. She winced as she appeared on screen, she looked so…small.

Her patient was a forty-five-year-old woman. Within a minute of entering the consulting room she was telling Erin that she was a single working mother, that she had three children, that she could cope very well without a man, thank you, that she enjoyed and was good at her job. She had pains in her chest.

'Do you smoke, Mrs Venn?'

'How else am I to get through the day? I need something to calm my nerves.'

Erin saw herself listen to Mrs Venn's heart and lungs, remembered the crackle she had heard. She had been pretty sure of her diagnosis, but had arranged for the woman to have her chest X-rayed just to double-check. Then she said, 'You've got some congestion in your lungs and I can give you something for that. Your heartbeat is a bit fast and your blood pressure is up. I'd like you to come back in a week or so and have it tested again. But you know yourself what the problem is, don't you?'

'It's my lifestyle. I try to do too much. And I've got to give up smoking. I've tried, but it's hard.'

Erin had printed out a prescription for a linctus, and then spent ten minutes discussing the alternatives to smoking—nicotine gum, a nicotine patch, attendance at the practice stop-smoking clinic. And Mrs Venn had left promising to give things a try.

'Well,' Cal said, 'let me say first of all that your examination was excellent and your diagnosis and prescription just what I'd have given. So was it a successful consultation?'

'No,' Erin said after a moment's thought. 'Mrs Venn got her linctus, but that's solved very little. The basic problem is her excessive smoking. And although I went through all the options with her, when I see her on camera, I can tell that she's not going to take any notice whatsoever.'

'Good. Now, she's a free agent, that's her own choice. But what might you have done to help her?'

'I could have been a bit more forceful. Told her about the possible later effects.'

'Exactly. It's not very often, but every now and again a patient needs waking up, given a scare even. This was such a case. Josh, what do you think?'

Josh looked apologetically at Erin. 'Could we see the first minute of the video again, please?'

Cal rewound it, played the first minute and Erin had to watch herself sitting at her desk and then greeting her patient. She didn't like it.

'Body language,' Josh said. 'Erin is crouched over her desk, she looks small, she doesn't…doesn't radiate confidence and efficiency. Once she gets talking, things improve, but that initial impression is a lasting one.'

Cal looked at her.

'Josh is right.' Erin nodded. 'I can see it.'

'So sit behind my desk here, Josh will come in as a patient and you try, as he says, to radiate confidence and efficiency.'

It was almost like playing a part, she could do it. And when Josh said, 'Well, you don't expect me to give up smoking, do you?' she was able to tell him much more forcibly of the dangers there were, and the treatments available.

At the end of the little scene Cal nodded approvingly.

'That was good,' he said. 'Now, d'you both feel you've learned something?'

They both had learned something.

'You're still a great actress,' Josh said as they drank coffee together later. 'Did you do any amateur theatricals when you were training?'

'A bit here and there. In my first three years I was in the drama society and I did the usual Christmas bits for the medical students. But…nothing for the past two years.'

'A pity. You were talented. I remember you in *The Rivals* before *Romeo and Juliet*, and you were a terrifying Lady Macbeth.'

She looked at him in surprise. 'You remember everything I was in!'

He turned slightly red. 'That shows how memorable your performances were. I enjoyed watching you.'

'It was just that we had a really encouraging drama mistress, Miss Cole. Remember her?'

'Who could forget her? But I think you were convincing because you were good at it. Have you ever thought of doing any again?'

No, she hadn't. Acting for her was now just not possible. But she wasn't going to tell him why. 'I think I'm too busy,' she said.

He changed the subject. 'I've got a favour to ask,' he said. 'Remember how I told you that I was player and doctor alternately at the rugby club? Well, they've asked me to play on Saturday, but they'd really like a doctor as well. There will be three games being played on the home ground. Would you come and be doctor? The chances are that you won't be needed. There's a tiny fee, and afterwards there'll be a free meal and as much beer as you can drink.'

'Who could resist such an invitation? Of course I'll come. But if it's raining, I want to borrow your umbrella.'

Of course, it did rain. She was dressed in her boots, anorak and jeans. But Josh had told her that they would have a drink in the bar afterwards and that, yes, he supposed that the other women there would 'dress up a bit'—so she took a case with something reasonably smart to change into.

Josh drove her to the rugby ground, introduced her to the trainer who showed her the first-aid room and assured her that he could deal with most of the injuries expected. 'You're here for anything major.' That made her feel slightly nervous, and determined, if necessary, to have Josh pulled off the field.

Rather to her surprise, she enjoyed watching the match. Many of the players were great beefy fellows, and Josh seemed almost slim in comparison—but he wasn't. With her heart in her mouth she watched him chase a man who must have weighed eighteen stone, tackle him and bring him crashing down. Josh was fast.

Later on she watched him make a great run down what she learned was the wing, and in a great maul of players apparently score a try. She cheered with all the other spectators. Then the referee ran up, there was some kind of discussion, and for some reason the try was disallowed. There was much irritation among the spectators around her.

About five minutes from the end of the game the trainer tapped her on the shoulder. Could she come to one of the other matches? A man had been tackled, had

had difficulty getting up and now was complaining of chest pains. Feeling rather apprehensive, Erin trotted after the trainer.

There was a knot of anxious players gathered round the fallen player. It seemed odd, to examine a man who was wet through and covered in mud. Very properly, he had been wrapped in a space blanket to keep him warm. She knelt by his side, noticed the paleness of his face under the grime.

'Hi, I'm Dr Erin Hunter. Tell me about this pain.'

'Good afternoon, Doctor. I'm Mike Snow. Nothing much to report. I was enjoying myself, was tackled quite fairly and fell in a bit of a heap. When I tried to get up I felt this pain in my chest—here.' He pointed to his side. 'It was moderately agonising so I decided that I'd like to stay put.'

'Only moderately agonising?' Erin asked, trying to hide her smile. 'Are you in any pain now?'

'Not too much, if I don't move.'

He had a cultured voice, which seemed to go oddly with his muddy state. Erin guessed that he'd be about fifty and noted that he was carrying just a little too much weight.

'Have you had any chest pains of this kind before, Mike? Any unexplained breathlessness?'

'Nothing like that. I'm a farmer, I keep reasonably fit. I don't think this is a heart attack.'

'We have to consider everything,' Erin said.

She checked his pulse, noted the breathing, then eased up the man's shirt and listened with her stethoscope. The heart was beating fast, of course—but there was absolutely nothing to worry about.

'You were right about the heart attack—you haven't had one. Now, if I can get my arm in here...' She slid her hand under the muddy shirt, felt down to where Mike had indicated the pain was. 'Does that hurt?' she asked.

'Quite considerably.'

Erin felt a little more, then withdrew her hand. 'When you were tackled, was there anything or anyone underneath you?'

'Could have been someone's leg that I fell on. It was all a bit of a mess.'

'I think you've broken a couple of ribs. We'll get you back to the first-aid room and I'll strap them up, then you'd better go to hospital for an X-ray. You should be all right, but we don't want a broken end piercing a lung or anything like that.'

'Not a good idea,' Mike agreed.

The trainer had sent for a stretcher, and under Erin's supervision Mike was carefully lifted onto it. Then he was carried to the first-aid room and the trainer phoned for an ambulance. Erin gave Mike a couple of strong painkillers as under the dirt his face was now a pasty grey colour. Then she cut away the shirt and gently washed the affected area.

'I'm not going to wash all of you,' she told Mike as she strapped up his ribs with a great roll of plaster. 'I'm leaving that to a nurse at the hospital.'

'Something to look forward to.'

'Broken ribs seem a hard price to pay for a bit of tender loving care. Besides, it might be a male nurse.' She pulled the blanket round him. 'Now, you lie there and keep warm and quiet. We don't want you going into shock.'

'Everything all right, Dr Hunter? Need a hand?'

Erin turned. A tremendously filthy Josh was standing, still in his kit, in the doorway. It was hard to tell, but she thought he was grinning.

'Everything's fine, thank you, Dr Harrison,' she said coolly. 'I can cope. There was absolutely no need for you to interrupt your game.'

'I have every confidence in your medical abilities.' He stepped further into the room and she saw that the trainer was supporting him with an arm round his waist and that he was limping. 'I didn't leave the game to come to help you.'

'Are you hurt, too?' Her voice sounded high and anxious, she was rather surprised at that. 'Josh, are you all right?'

Now she could see him clearly. There was the bulge of a dressing inside his right sock and above his ankle the darkness that suggested blood rather than mud.

'I got my right calf gashed in a maul, probably someone hacking for the ball a bit too enthusiastically. It's bleeding quite a bit but there's nothing to worry about.'

'I'll decide what's to worry about. I'm the doctor, you're the patient. Lie on that bench and keep warm.' She turned back to Mike. 'Suddenly we're busy. Give me a call if you feel any worse.'

He's just a patient, Erin said to herself as she crossed the room to where Josh was lying, he's just a patient and you're his doctor. You've worked in A and E before, you know how to distance yourself, how to keep your emotions in check. But it was difficult. She realised she just didn't want Josh to be hurt. He was too precious to her.

Gently, she pulled down the muddy sock, lifted the temporary dressing that had been pressed against the gash. 'It's nasty,' she said. 'It's long but it's quite shallow. I don't think we need to suture it, butterfly stitches will do. But there's a lot of dirt in the cut, we'll have to clean you up a bit. I take it you are up to date with your tetanus jabs?'

'Yes, Doctor,' he said mildly.

'Then I'll fetch a bowl of water and we'll clean you up.'

She concentrated on the cut, trying to forget that this muscular leg belonged to a man who was—well, she was realising he had become more than her friend. If she stopped being a doctor for a minute she knew that she would feel a chaos of inexplicable emotions—and she didn't want that.

Erin cleaned the cut, fixed it with butterfly stitches and then covered everything with a waterproof dressing. 'Can you get yourself clean without getting the dressing too wet?'

'There's a bath I can use. I'll hang my leg over the side. Thank you, Doctor, that was a professional bit of work.' He swung himself upright on the bench, then limped out of the room.

Erin went back to her other patient. Josh was now dealt with, she would forget him. 'How old are you, Mike?' she asked.

'Fifty-five next birthday.'

'You don't think that perhaps you ought to be slowing down a bit? This game takes it out of you.'

'You mean stop rugby and play golf or something? I'd rather...' Mike coughed, and then grimaced with pain. 'Well, this was going to be my last season,' he went on. 'But I don't want to stop now that it's started. I think when you start something you should finish it.'

'I know someone who sounds just like you. He can get into trouble, too. Now, make sure you have a thorough check-up before you start playing again.'

Through the frosted window she could see a white

vehicle drawing up. The ambulance had arrived. 'I'm handing you over now. See you again, Mike.'

Josh had told her that it would take him perhaps three-quarters of an hour to bath, change and then have a sandwich with members of the visiting teams. 'If you don't mind waiting, perhaps we could have a drink in the bar afterwards.'

'I'd like that. And I've brought something to change into myself. I'm not going to sit in a bar with muddy stains on my trouser knees.'

So, after she had seen Mike transferred into the ambulance, she went into the ladies' changing room, put on a grey silk dress and her high heels, and saw to her hair. She had noticed one or two of the other girls arriving, none of them in jeans and sweater. This was now a social occasion.

Rather shyly, she made her way to the bar. As she entered, a smart, white-haired older gentleman in a blue blazer came over to greet her. 'Dr Hunter? Dr Harrison asked me to look out for you, I'm Colonel Ward, the club president. May I thank you for being our doctor today and get you a drink? And we can have a sandwich together.'

'Thank you. I think I'd like a glass of red wine.'

Erin thought she was being treated very well, this was different from the casual way she had been treated when she'd been doctor at other functions. She sat with the colonel in a corner and watched the bar fill up.

Then, just when she was questioning the colonel about the age of the club players, she looked up—and there was Josh.

He was wearing the same uniform as the rest of the

players, grey flannels, white shirt and the club blue
blazer and tie. He looked very smart.

'Leave you two together, then,' the colonel said when
he, too, saw Josh. 'Hope to see you at a match again,
Dr Hunter. Have a good evening.' And he was gone.

'I've got myself a pint,' Josh said. 'And I've brought
you another glass of red wine.'

His face was slightly pink from the bath, his hair still
wet. There was a graze on his cheekbone. And Erin
thought that he looked gorgeous. She moved so he could
sit by her side.

'How's the leg?'

'It's throbbing a bit. But I'm going to be fine, I have
a great doctor.'

'Flattery will get you nowhere.' She decided to
change the subject. 'You're wearing a blue blazer and
grey flannels,' she said. 'I don't ever remember you
looking like this when you were at school.'

'Looking like what?' he asked.

Her face warmed and she didn't reply. 'I gather you
lost the match,' she said instead, 'though it was very
close. What was that trouble near the end? I thought you
had scored a try.'

He laughed, rather self-consciously. 'I'm afraid I
nearly lost a couple of friends as well as the match. You
know that to score a try, the ball has to go over the line
and actually be touched to the ground? Well, I got over
the line, tried to touch down and was hauled back before
I could do so. The referee didn't see that I hadn't
touched down and was going to award the try. So I told
him what had happened and he disallowed it.'

'But he would have allowed it if you hadn't told him?'

'Yes. And in effect it lost us the game.'

'So why did you tell him?'

He shrugged. 'It's a game, Erin. If you don't play by the rules, why play at all?'

She thought about that. 'You're quite tough on the quiet, aren't you?' she said.

After that they talked about how their medical training had differed, how old their cottages might be, why were there always women in rugby clubs willing to come in on Saturday afternoons and make sandwiches. Three or four other men in blazers strolled over to be introduced and chat for a while, so obviously Josh hadn't irritated everyone. Erin was really enjoying herself. There was a warm, a relaxed atmosphere about the place, she felt among friends.

Then someone walked in the door and Erin's happiness evaporated.

She put her hand on Josh's arm, pulled him towards her. 'Lean forward,' she muttered. 'There's someone there I just don't want to see me.'

Josh looked round. 'Who? If there's trouble I can sort it out.'

'Not that kind of trouble, and you couldn't sort it out. You men! It's a woman and I just don't want her to see me.'

But it was too late, she had been spotted. A thin, unsmiling woman came over and stood for a moment looking at them. 'Hello, Erin, I didn't expect to see you back here. I thought you'd turned your back on us for good.'

'Hello, Mrs King,' Erin said flatly.

'Come here to settle now, have you?'

'I'm a registrar at the local practice. I'll be here for a year and then I'm going back to London. I have a job waiting.'

'I see.' Mrs King's thin lips grew even thinner. 'Will

you be dropping in to see David? If you have time, that is.'

'I think I'll be calling,' Erin said. 'As you say, when I have time.'

Mrs King glanced round the bar, then stared at Josh. 'Yes. I can see you are busy now, so I'll leave you.'

There was a moment's frozen silence and then the woman turned and left the room.

With an unsteady hand Erin reached for her glass. The wine didn't taste as it had done two minutes before. She had enjoyed her afternoon, had enjoyed her evening in the bar. And now it was spoiled. She'd known she would have to face Mrs King some time—and her son. This was partly why she had come back to the Lake District. But she wasn't ready yet.

'Am I mistaken, or did the atmosphere get a little chilly there?' Josh asked.

Another problem. She had to offer some kind of explanation to Josh. And she didn't want to.

'Mrs King and I have had our disagreements,' Erin said.

'I see.' He looked at her thoughtfully. 'Mrs King? Is she some relation to David King? The one I was rather jealous of?'

'There has never been any reason for you to be jealous of David King,' she snapped.

Quickly, she finished her wine, then stood. 'I just don't want to talk about it, Josh, and it certainly doesn't concern you. Now, you stay here and enjoy yourself with your friends and I'll ring for a taxi. I've had a very good day but I think it's time I left.'

He stood, too, drank the rest of his beer and set the glass on the table with a determined clink. She recognised his expression, it was one she had seen before.

When he decided to wait to catch their car thief he had looked this way. He was going to do what he thought was right—no matter what the cost.

'You have every right not to talk if you don't want to,' he said softly, 'and I wouldn't dream of pushing you. But it does concern me when you're in trouble because we work together and I think we're getting to be far more than friends. You are in trouble, aren't you?'

'Nothing I can't handle myself.'

'Then I'll say nothing more, except that I'd like to help if I can. As for going home in a taxi, my leg hurts a bit and I'm going home myself. Don't argue, I'm taking you.'

Erin knew better than to argue. 'All right,' she said.

It would be quite early when they arrived home. The evening had come to an early end, it would seem strange for them to part politely and each go to their respective homes. So she said, 'I don't want a late night. But if you'd like to come in for an hour or so, you'd be very welcome. There's a beef and bean casserole slow-cooking in the oven—we could share it.'

'That would be great. Man cannot live on sandwiches alone. Just one thing, can I fetch a bottle of wine? I've laid in a stock.'

'It'd better be red with beef,' she said.

While he was next door, fetching the wine, she quickly slipped out of her dress and put on a T-shirt and a pair of comfortable trousers. When he returned he had taken off his blazer and tie so they were both more comfortable.

Perhaps she was tired. Certainly Josh must be. Whatever it was, they were both completely relaxed. The tensions of the day appeared to have drained away and they were quietly happy to sit there together.

The casserole was cooked to perfection. She split a French loaf and grilled it because she didn't have time to cook potatoes. And they sat at her kitchen table and ate, then took their glasses into her tiny living room.

'That was different from my student meal,' Josh said comfortably. 'That was haute cuisine. What I gave you was catering.'

'It was very welcome, comfort eating. I've got a student meal myself.'

They were sitting side by side on her couch. Usually in the evening she tried to watch the news on TV, but tonight she just didn't feel like it.

There was something she had to ask him. 'In the bar in the rugby club,' she said, 'I was a bit upset and angry. And you said something to me that I should have replied to, and I didn't.'

Their shoulders were touching—she felt his muscles tense and then relax. But his voice remained calm. 'What was that?' he asked.

She swallowed. This wasn't as hard as she had expected. The food, the wine and his company had calmed her. But it was still quite hard to say. 'You said that we were getting to be more than friends.'

He took her hand, stroked the back of it with his thumb. It was a tiny caress but it gave her much pleasure.

'I think we are getting to be more than friends. I know that both of us are cautious, wary of any involvement. I don't want to make any great declaration now. I want to wait to see what happens. But I spend a lot of time thinking about you. You light up the room when you come into it. I can't think of anywhere I'd rather be than here with you now.'

'That's a lovely thing to say. But hearing it is a bit of a responsibility. Josh, I…I like you a lot. But I've got a lot of emotional baggage and I need time to…to get things straight.' She knew the last few words sounded lame and unconvincing. But he didn't seem to mind.

'We have time,' he said. 'I can be patient—though sometimes it's hard. Now—serious talk at an end?'

'Serious talk at an end. And I do like you being here with me.' She wriggled closer to him, rested her head on his shoulder.

Afterwards, Erin couldn't understand it. It wasn't what she wanted—at least not yet. Josh had said he was willing to wait. They both were wary, neither of them wanted any kind of commitment yet.

She remembered that flash of attraction when they had first met. She had dismissed it as purely physical. Perhaps what had happened had been purely physical. But she doubted it. They were attracted to each other whether they wanted to be or not.

When she laid her head on his shoulder she felt his body stiffen. But then he relaxed and she snuggled closer. She put one arm round his waist—it seemed a warm thing to do. And he slipped his arm round her shoulders and drew her closer.

For longer than she could imagine they stayed like that, each at ease, each comfortable. When they spoke, they talked vaguely of their training, their plans for the future. Most of the time they were content to remain silent.

But slowly, inexorably, she came to know that things must change. Perhaps it was her head, so close to his heart, feeling the steady thud of his pulse. Perhaps she felt his breathing grow shallower, more rapid. Whatever it was, it affected her, too.

He slid down the couch and kissed her. Their heads were together, he touched his lips to hers with infinite gentleness. His arm was still holding her, but with a touch so light that she knew she could break free at once—if she wished.

She stared into his dark green eyes, wondering what she could read there. Nothing. His gaze was unfathomable. So she closed her own eyes and surrendered to the pleasure of his kiss.

His grip tightened on her. Now both his arms were round her and she wanted him to pull her closer to him, press his body against hers. She wanted all of him. Now his lips were demanding, and she gave way at once, opening her mouth to the insistent pressure of his, tasting the sweetness of him. Her hands tore at his shirt, pulling it away from him so she could stroke her fingers across the skin of his back, the muscles rippling across his abdomen.

A vague, distant part of her brain said that this wasn't a good idea, that there were things to be settled first. She ignored it.

Now his hand slipped across her waistband, insinuated itself under her T-shirt and trailed slowly upwards. Dimly she realised why he was moving so slowly. If she wanted, she could stop him at any time. But she didn't want to stop him. His fingertips gave her so much pleasure.

His other hand was now behind her, and with thumb and finger he undid the hook of her bra. She sighed with the feeling of freedom, and then sobbed with pleasure as he took her breast in his hand, stroked the throbbing tip into excitement.

For a while that was enough—more than enough. But then, with an incomprehensible word of explanation, she eased him away from her, crossed her arms and drew the white top over her head. T-shirt and discarded bra fell to the floor. He lowered his head, took her breast in his mouth and she arched her back in ecstasy. 'So long,' she heard him gasp after a while. 'I've waited so long.'

She knew that there could be only one possible end to this, and she yearned for it. Consequences were unimportant. All that mattered to her was this moment, and the feelings he was arousing in her. Feverishly he kissed her lips, then bent his head to her breasts again. She called out with the pleasure of it, her head jerking backwards, her legs thrust out in excitement.

Her coffee-table was a handsome piece of furniture, a great slab of heavy green slate, mounted on stout oak legs. Erin kicked it, wine bottle and glasses crashed to the floor. And somehow the table itself rocked and fell. The hard edge of slate slammed into Josh's leg—just where he had gashed it.

She felt rather than heard his cry of pain. His arms, wrapped so tightly round her, jerked with the shock. His lips were torn from her breasts. She knew at once what had happened, gathered him to her in an embrace that now was meant to comfort rather than to excite. And they held each other like that till his breathing eased.

She looked at his face, which was white with pain. 'I'd better look at your leg,' she said. She knelt in front of him, pulled up his trouser leg. Fresh blood was oozing from behind the dressing. 'You need a new bandage, I'll get one.'

As she walked to the kitchen she scooped up her T-shirt and bra. It was time to get dressed again.

When she returned he had picked up the bottle and glasses. Fortunately they weren't broken and since they had been empty there were no stains on the carpet. He was sitting on the couch, his face sombre. Whatever had been between them before had now gone. She thought that they felt like two strangers.

She knelt in front of him, carefully peeled off the old dressing and washed the wound again. A couple of the butterfly stitches had come apart and she replaced them. Performing the simple medical tasks helped settle her fast-beating heart. 'That's done,' she said eventually. 'I kicked the table onto your leg. I'm sorry.'

'This is not a good time to allocate blame,' he said. 'Erin, could I ask you for a cup of coffee?'

'I'll make a pot for both of us.' She fled to the kitchen again.

She made the coffee strong, very strong, and when she returned she sat opposite him in an easy chair. They drank their coffee in silence and then he said, 'I must apologise for—'

'You must apologise for nothing! Whatever happened was with my complete consent. I was just as guilty as you...if guilt is the right word.'

Josh shook his head. 'I wasn't going to apologise for what I did. For a start it would be hypocritical. You've no idea what pleasure you gave me. It was the realisation of years of dreaming, it was wonderful.'

'I liked it, too,' she said. 'So why are you apologising?'

'Because I was unfair to you. We're not ready yet. What happened just now was too physical,' he said, the words rushing out. 'My body enjoyed it no end, my brain—my soul if you like—told me that there was much more we need to sort out first. Erin, neither of us is ready for a loving relationship. We don't know each other well enough.'

'I take it you're not interested in a purely physical relationship?' she asked, her mouth dry. 'Sex together but no strings?'

'No, I'm not interested in that kind of relationship,' he said irritably. 'And don't play games, Erin. You're not interested in that kind of thing either.'

'No,' she said after a while. 'No, I'm not. So where do we go now?'

He stood. 'I go home, next door. And if you don't think that's hard, you're wrong. I hope that when we meet next that we'll still be able to be professionals together and we can try to build something between us that will be longer-lasting. What happened this evening will be forgotten.'

She stood silent a moment. Then she said, 'What happened this evening can be ignored, never referred to, forgiven if necessary. But some things once they have occurred, can never be forgotten. This was one of them.'

'I'm so sorry,' he said. Then he stood and limped to the door.

When he had gone Erin sat motionless for half an hour. Then she jumped to her feet, went to the kitchen and cleared away the few dishes they had used. The glasses they had used were washed, the covers of the couch pulled straight, she even squirted air freshener into the living room. If she put her head close to the soft covers of the couch there was no scent of his after-shave—or indeed, of him.

But it wasn't enough. It was as if he was still with her, in the air that swirled around her. Suddenly she remembered, pulled up the front of her T-shirt and smelled that. He was there, too. She ripped off the offending garment, stuffed it straight in the washing machine. And then all trace of him had been wiped from her home. Would it be as easy to wipe him from her life?

She decided on a traditional remedy. She ran a hot deep bath, threw in a liberal amount of expensive foaming bath salts, and then cautiously slipped into the water. For a while she was content just to lie there, feeling as if she were being cooked. But slowly the heat and the scents calmed her and she was able to think about what had happened.

Now she had trouble with two men—and she didn't need it. She had her career to think of, a life in front of her.

What was she to do about Josh? She had to be brutally honest with herself. This evening, wherever he had wanted to lead her, she would have followed. He could have led her to bed—hers or his own. But tonight had been an accident, a one-off, it wouldn't happen again. They had agreed earlier that they might come to mean something to each other, but it would take time. She didn't want an instant new relationship—and neither apparently did he. Fair enough. Now they understood each other they could work well together.

But even as she decided that the matter was settled, a disturbing voice whispered to her that life was never that simple.

CHAPTER FOUR

NEXT day was Sunday. Josh hadn't been able to sleep very well and woke early. There was work he had to do but he wasn't on call at the practice so he decided the only way he could calm himself was by walking. Climbing a mountain would put everything into perspective. And besides, the sun was shining through his window, today looked as if the weather would be glorious.

He stepped out of bed. And when he tried to stand up, something sharp apparently stabbed him in the leg. He had forgotten, and he looked down at the dressing still on his calf. Erin had told him, and he knew very well himself, that the cut would heal quickly. But only if he took things easy for a few days. A hard walk was impossible. But he had to get out, to clear his brain somehow.

Eventually he got into his car, drove over the tops to Keswick. He parked by the lake and limped over to the little marina. He was the first to hire a rowing boat for that morning. It would be a good way to get some exercise without straining his leg.

Derwentwater was a still blue mirror, the peaks surrounding it reflected in its depths. At first he rowed strongly, trying to work up a rhythm, trying to find peace in exercise. But then assorted other little aches and pains reminded him that yesterday he had played a hard game of rugby. It was possible to overdo it. So in the middle of the lake he shipped his oars and was content to sit there, a tiny figure in a boat, surrounded by majesty.

He thought about Erin. And after a while it struck him that he had been selfish. He had worried solely about himself, about his growing feelings for Erin. He had thought of her only in relation to himself. But now he was realising that she had problems of her own.

She looked different. Once she had walked proudly, blue eyes keen and searching. Now she seemed almost fearful. Her long blonde hair was scraped back. She was still the beauty she had always been—but now she wasn't confident with it.

There had been hints, indications that he should have picked up on. Most recently, what was her quarrel with Mrs King? The woman seemed to hate her. Why was Erin so reluctant to be called Juliet, to look back at her schooldays with happiness? Josh could remember the last day of the production of *Romeo and Juliet*. He had seen her come to the front of the stage and receive a bouquet of flowers, she had been radiant. Why should she want to forget that?

And in general there was an edginess to her. She was good at her work and obviously enjoyed it. But she lacked confidence. She had always been confident. Something had scared her.

More thoughtfully, Josh took up his oars and started to row back to the marina. There were others in the world with problems besides himself. He wondered if he could help her. Certainly he wanted to. But, then, whatever was wrong, he suspected she was not going to tell him.

Josh felt calmer when he got back home. It was still early, there was work to do, but he thought he could approach it more easily now. He didn't know what he had decided but he thought he had decided something.

As he opened the front door the telephone rang. He frowned. He wasn't on duty. Who else could call him? His heart bumped as he wondered if it could be Erin. He walked over to the phone and picked it up.

The voice was confident, educated, but with perhaps just a touch of anxiety to it. 'Dr Harrison? I don't know if you remember me, we haven't met for many years but we were at school together. My name is David King.'

'I do remember you,' Josh said briefly. 'You played Romeo.'

'How kind of you to remember. That was a long time ago. The thing is, Dr Harrison, I was wondering if you could come round to see me. As soon as possible. This afternoon would be ideal.'

'I'm not on call this afternoon. If this is an emergency, you can ring the surgery and they'll arrange for someone to come round.'

David laughed—rather a forced laugh, Josh thought. 'Oh, this isn't a medical emergency. Well, only indirectly a medical emergency. I think it's more a personal thing.'

'Can you give me some idea of what kind of personal thing?'

'Not over the phone. We need to talk face to face. Please, come, Dr Harrison. I'm sure you'll find what I have to say of interest.'

Josh hesitated. He didn't like David's tone. There was a touch of something—was it hysteria there? But the man had intrigued him, and he knew he would have to go.

'I can get there this afternoon but I won't have much time. About two o'clock?'

'Excellent. I live with my mother. It's a big house off the Windermere road, you turn off—'

'I know the house. It's called Longfell View.'

'You know it, good. Just one thing more, Dr Harrison. Could you keep your visit to yourself until we've spoken? It might avoid embarrassment all round.'

'I can't see myself being embarrassed, I've got nothing to be embarrassed about. But I'll do as you ask.'

Josh replaced the phone and frowned. He had a suspicion he was being manoeuvred into something and he didn't know what. He didn't like the feeling, and he realised he hadn't liked David's voice. Well, whatever it was, he'd know soon enough.

He'd never visited Longfell View when he'd been at school as he hadn't moved in David King's circle, but the house had been pointed out to him. It was the home of a rich man—or woman, apparently.

The gardens were immaculately kept. The house itself was built of traditional grey stone and slate. He liked it at first. But as Josh drew up outside the front door he thought that if it had been his house he would have had the window-frames replaced with wood, instead of the plastic that someone had chosen. Well, it wasn't his house.

'Dr Harrison, it's good of you to come. Could I get you some tea?' It was Mrs King who answered the door.

'Tea would be fine, thank you.' Josh wondered if he was getting paranoid. Was there something sneaky about Mrs King's manner? It seemed as if she knew something that he didn't, something that was going to cause him pain. And the thought pleased her.

'David is through here. He asked to see you at once.' Josh was led down a panelled corridor into a large living room. He noticed a large television set, an expensive hifi system, stacks of CDs and videos. Near them David was lying on a couch, his legs covered by a tartan rug.

'Josh! You haven't changed in ten years.' David held out his hand but didn't attempt to stand.

Josh shook the outstretched hand briefly. 'Neither have you.'

That wasn't entirely true. David still had his film-star good looks, but he hadn't aged well. There were petulant lines down the sides of his cheeks, it looked as if he frowned a lot.

Josh took the chair indicated for him. 'How can I help you, David?'

David looked at him assessingly. 'I want to talk to you about Erin Hunter,' he said, 'and about this.'

With an overly dramatic gesture he swept away the rug covering his legs. Josh looked down—and somehow managed not to wince. He remembered David King as a lithe, graceful figure, capering about the stage in the tightest of white tights. David would never do so again. His right leg had been amputated below the knee.

There was silence for a moment. Then Josh said, 'I'm truly sorry to see you've been injured so badly, David. But how does it concern Erin Hunter—or me for that matter?'

'My mother saw you with Erin at the rugby club yesterday. It was the first I knew she was here. She didn't see fit to tell me that she had moved back into the area.'

'Why should she?'

David smiled bitterly. 'Because we are—I think—engaged.' He reached to a table, took up a small box and opened it. 'This is her engagement ring.'

Josh looked at him, unable to speak.

'I've brought your tea,' Mrs King said, entering with a tray. 'Do you take sugar, Dr Harrison?'

'Shouldn't she be wearing the ring?' Josh asked when Mrs King had left. 'That's the custom, isn't it?'

David shrugged. 'There are reasons, I'll explain them to you. Hasn't Erin ever spoken to you about me?'

'No,' Josh said slowly. 'Whenever I mentioned you, or wanted to talk about the school play, she got a bit angry. Said she didn't want go over old ground.'

'Denial.' David shook his head. 'She doesn't want to admit it now. You know we kept in touch constantly after we both left school? I take it you didn't?'

'No. My parents moved to a farm down south. I never had cause to come back here. I hadn't seen Erin in nearly ten years.' Josh couldn't tell why, but this news seemed to please David.

'Well, Erin and I saw a lot of each other. She was training to be a doctor, I was training to be a solicitor. It was generally agreed that in time we'd get married. I'd even bought this ring.'

David's voice grew harsher. Instead of looking at Josh, he stared out of the window. 'Just under two years ago we were up here, and went walking together. We started to climb Helvellyn and halfway up I took out the ring and asked her to marry me. She said yes and tried the ring on, but it was too big, it kept slipping off her finger. So I kept it in my pocket. Then she said she wanted to walk along Striding Edge to celebrate. There was snow on the ground, it was icy, we didn't have the proper kit, but if that's what she wanted I was willing to go along with it.'

He paused, as if trying to keep his voice calm. 'Well, we fell. A really bad fall. They had to turn out the mountain rescue team for us, carry us down on stretchers. Her head was hurt, I smashed up my leg. There were complications, an infection—and my leg had to be amputated.'

Now he was obviously fighting back the tears. 'All I had to hang onto was the fact that I had Erin. But when eventually she did come to see me she saw my amputated leg and said we would just be friends. She claimed that we were never engaged. But I showed her the ring!'

There was silence for a moment, and now it was Josh's turn to stare out of the window to give David time to calm himself. Eventually he said, 'I feel sorry, really I do. But this was some time ago. Haven't you been fitted with a prosthesis yet?'

David shrugged. 'Artificial legs. They're useless. I've tried them, got nowhere.'

'I would have thought you could have been walking by now. Have you had counselling?'

'I've had lots of people trying to help me and none of them has done any good.'

'I see.' Josh was finding this meeting more and more unpleasant. 'One thing, David, why did you want to tell me all this?'

'I told you, my mother saw you with Erin last night. You seemed to be quite close and I thought this was something you should know. If you don't mind my asking, just what is your relationship with her?'

'That is for her to decide. She'll tell you if she wants you to know.'

'But I never see her! She promised to come and see me but she's never been! Will you tell her that I'd like her to come and see me?'

'Your relationship with Erin has nothing to do with me,' Josh said coldly. 'Now, thank you for your concern, but I have calls to make.' He rose.

'Just a minute! You're not my doctor, we go privately,

but I have been feeling rather sick recently. A gastric upset. D'you think you could examine me, perhaps prescribe something? I'd pay, of course, it'd be a purely personal thing.'

'I'm sorry, that would be unprofessional. You don't look ill to me, but if you are, then call out your own doctor. Goodbye, David.'

David said nothing as Josh walked to the door.

Mrs King was waiting outside, ready to see him out. 'Will we see you again, Dr Harrison? David gets so few visitors.'

Josh had a good idea that she had been listening at the door. He said briefly, 'I doubt I'll be calling again. I'm kept very busy and we have little in common. Good afternoon, Mrs King.'

Never had the sun felt so good on his face. He drove away, perhaps faster than was safe, until the house was far behind him. Then he took a side road, followed it upwards until the open fells spread before him. He got out of the car and limped for half a mile until he was far from any humans. Then he lay on the sheep-cropped grass and tried desperately to make sense of the scene he had just endured.

First, he was a doctor and he had just refused to treat—or at least examine—someone who had asked for help. But this worry was soon overcome. David didn't really need his help, he had just been trying to keep Josh with him for a few minutes more. Then something else struck Josh. If he had treated David, then David would have become one of his patients. And he wasn't allowed to discuss or pass on any medical information about a patient.

Josh smiled wryly to himself. He suspected that

David, in a very cunning way, had been trying to gag him.

But David wasn't the problem—the problem was Erin.

Josh had decided that after Annabelle for a while he would be wary of further emotional contact with women. They just weren't worth the pain, the conflict. If he had been so wrong about Annabelle, then almost certainly he would be wrong about the next girl. Better to keep them at a distance, or keep them solely as friends.

It was a pity that, after Annabelle, the first girl that he had come in contact with had been Erin. She made Annabelle seem tawdry. Slowly, in time, perhaps he and Erin could form something that was much more permanent. And then, last night, for reasons he just couldn't explain, they had nearly...

So much for my strength of character, he mused bitterly. But I'll do better in future.

Now, how had what David told him altered his view of Erin? David's story was all too possibly plausible. There was the ring, the amputated leg, the fact that Erin seemed angry—or embarrassed—or guilty—every time David's name was mentioned. She must have something to hide.

Josh frowned. This was a side of Erin he hadn't suspected, one he didn't like. To reject a man when he needed love and support most was more than selfish. And yet that's what Erin appeared to have done. He wanted nothing to do with such a woman.

Still, he mustn't judge her, not yet. There were a hundred ways of telling a story, her way might be different. He would have to ask—although it might be hard.

He walked back to his car. His leg ached a little where he had gashed it. He remembered the night before, when

Erin had knelt in front of him, replacing the dressing. The bowed shoulders, the tightly bound blonde hair had stirred his emotions in a way he had not expected. And now he was more confused than ever.

Cal had quite an extensive practice library and all the staff used it frequently. Josh turned first to the sections that dealt with amputations. As he knew, the surgical procedure was relatively uncomplicated. He looked also at amputations resulting from infection, and found they were more common than he had suspected.

Next he looked at the sections that dealt with prostheses—specifically artificial legs. This merely reinforced what he already know, that a determined young man could have an incredible amount of mobility if he persevered with his training.

And, last, he turned to the sections dealing with the psychological effects of losing a limb. Most people coped, some doing very well indeed. A few just could not come to terms with the problem. Family support was all-important. And if a family member or close friend showed signs of distress or repugnance, the effects could be catastrophic.

Josh closed his eyes, thinking of David. He just hadn't liked the man, he seemed self-pitying and manipulative. Then Josh wondered how he'd feel himself if he lost a leg. He'd like to think he'd be strong, resilient, come to terms with the situation. But a bit of the horror peeped through. And if someone you loved didn't support you… Someone like Erin?

On that Sunday Erin had risen early, taken her car and gone for a long drive through the countryside. She knew she'd have to meet Josh again, they had to work together and they'd patch something up somehow. But not just yet. There was no light on in his cottage when she arrived back home.

First thing Monday she drove down to the Leeds medical school. There she had a series of lectures and seminars on GP training, and learned quite a lot. Cal had arranged a series of visits, a necessary part of her training.

It was fun to mix with a large group again. But in the coffee-breaks and over lunch, she came to realise just how lucky she was in working for the Keldale practice. Her conditions and the people she had to deal with were the envy of many. 'You don't get that kind of life working in the city centre,' one man said enviously. 'I've had my car smashed four times so far.'

She found she was glad to leave the suburbs of Leeds behind, even more glad when she saw the hills of the Lake District appearing in outline in front of her. She felt she was coming home. Then she frowned. Until recently home to her had been London. When had she changed her mind?

Erin had been invited to drop into Cal's house that evening to have tea with him, Jane and Helen. Of course, she saw Cal and Jane practically every day but in spite of everyone's attempt to be friendly, this was primarily a professional relationship. It was good to see the family when they were relaxed.

Erin sat in the kitchen, Helen on her knee, as Jane bustled round, cooking.

Helen was Cal's and Jane's niece, her parents having been tragically killed. Cal and Jane were about to get married and then adopt her.

'I'm to be a bridesmaid,' Helen told Erin importantly.

'I'm to have a long dress and go to the hairdresser's and then have flowers in my hair. And some silver slippers. Do you think pink is a nice colour for a dress?'

'You'll look lovely in pink,' Erin told her. 'I always wanted to be a bridesmaid, but nobody ever asked me,'

'I'm going to keep my dress. Then if anyone else asks me to be a bridesmaid, I'll have the dress and I'll know what to do. You're not going to get married, are you, Erin? 'Cos I'll soon grow out of the dress.'

'No, I'm afraid I'm not getting married soon, I can't find anyone nice like Uncle Cal. But if I do, you can be my bridesmaid.'

'Auntie Jane, Auntie Jane, Erin says I can be her bridesmaid,' Helen shouted.

Jane turned, lifted her eyebrows in mock surprise. 'Anyone we know?' she asked with a grin. 'Isn't this a bit sudden?'

Erin blushed and then laughed. 'Helen forgot the first half of my sentence. I said she could be my bridesmaid if I found anyone nice, like Cal.'

Cal ambled into the kitchen. 'Anyone nice like me?' he asked. 'Tell me more about me being nice.'

Jane wrapped her arm round his waist and kissed his cheek. 'There is nobody as nice as you,' she said. 'Now, start slicing the bread.'

Cal winked at Erin. 'Just a skivvy,' he said. 'Would you treat a man this way, Erin?'

'If I had one, certainly. When is the wedding to be, Cal?'

'Very soon. Lyn is now pregnant and she and Adam want to get married, but we asked first. And all four of us met in the cottages you and Josh are living in. You don't think there's something catching in the air there, do you?'

'If there is, it hasn't infected me.'

'Give it time,' Jane said. 'Now, the salad's done, let's eat.'

They were such a close, happy family, Erin thought as she sat down at the table. Would she ever share in happiness like this?

'Why, it's Erin Hunter. Erin my dear, come in. It's so good to see you.'

'Hello, Miss Cole.' She stepped inside the cottage door. 'I didn't expect to find you here in the village.'

It was Tuesday morning, Cal had sent her across the village to look at a patient who had just had her hipbone replaced. 'She gets a regular visit from Jane,' he told her, 'and apparently there are no end of friends dropping in. But I like a doctor to see every patient from time to time. Don't worry, this isn't some kind of test.'

So Erin had set off across the village and to her surprise had met an old friend. Miss Cole had been her drama teacher and coach at school.

'I moved here when I retired,' Miss Cole said. 'I felt I needed a quieter life. But I don't seem to be having one.'

She turned and made her determined way down the corridor, assisted by her Zimmer frame. Erin was pleased to stay behind and watch her move. You could learn a lot by watching leg movements. And Miss Cole seemed to be doing fine.

Miss Cole also seemed quite happy to accept the reversal of roles, to let Erin examine her. This could be one of the less happy results of coming to be a doctor in a place where you had grown up. People who had known you as a child didn't like undressing in front of you or confessing their secrets. Cal had warned her about that.

'People's dignity is all-important to them, and as a doctor you must strive to preserve it. If you suspect someone doesn't want to be examined by you because they know you, then offer them another doctor. It's usually easy enough to arrange.'

But Miss Cole had no such qualms, and after Erin had looked at the rapidly healing wound and tested the range of movements, she had insisted that Erin stay for a cup of tea.

'I know you're a doctor now, but do you still do any acting, my dear? You did have a talent, you know, and I like to think that I helped bring it out.'

'I acted a bit in amateur productions at university and I enjoyed it. But a couple of years ago I had an accident...and it sort of knocked my confidence.'

'Nothing better than acting for bringing confidence back,' Miss Cole said, confident herself. 'You must join our local amateur group. We meet on a Thursday evening in the village hall. Could you manage that?'

Erin thought. At the moment medicine was all she did—she had no social life. Doing something else might be good for her. 'I'll come to the meetings when I can,' she said. 'But I don't want to appear on stage.'

'Of course not, dear,' Miss Cole said in the bland voice that suggested she intended to pay no attention whatsoever. 'Now, may I pour you another cup of tea?'

Erin met Josh for the first time since Saturday evening just outside her door when she got home. They were both about to go to the surgery for the evening appointments, so they walked together. She smiled at him cautiously, he looked at her in an assessing way. Perhaps he was worried that she didn't want to talk to him. Didn't he realise that they had to get on?

'Settling in all right?' he asked after they had paced several yards in silence. 'I hadn't been back for years, but I found people very friendly. A lot of them remembered me.'

'I'm settling in. And I've been back here quite a bit over the past few years.'

'Of course. See many of your old friends? See anything of David King?'

Had he heard? What did he know? She said, 'I've seen something of him. But not much over the past couple of years.'

When he spoke his voice was carefully neutral. 'I heard you were engaged to him. Were you?'

She felt the anger rising inside her. How dared he question her? This was her problem, the one she had come here to sort out. Josh was a sympathetic man and when she had felt a little more confident she would have confided in him. But she was not going to be pushed into a corner now.

'Possibly,' she said. 'Certainly not now. Is it any business of yours?'

'Of course not. I'm sorry I asked. I shan't mention it again.'

They were now at the door of the surgery and went their different ways. Erin felt a great ache inside her. Perhaps it was for the best. Perhaps the best relationship between them would be a kind of guarded neutrality. One thing was certain. By his body language, he didn't much care for her.

'Barry Keith,' Cal said to Erin and Josh next morning. 'He's seventy-nine, lives on his own in a place called

Dark End cottage. It's miles from anywhere, there are no neighbours and it should have been condemned years ago. But Barry likes it.'

He pushed over the case notes to them. 'Barry's got Alzheimer's disease and it's getting worse. I'd like you to read these notes then go to the cottage and meet a social worker called Cassie Beynon. She needs a decision on Barry's future.'

He frowned. 'I know most of the social workers but this is a new one, I've never met her. Apparently she's fresh out of college.'

'Just like us,' Erin said mischievously. 'Full of fine theories and no practical knowledge.'

'Shoo,' said Cal, waving his hand at them. 'If I meet any more young doctors I'll start to feel old. And if Barry offers you a drink, refuse.'

'Shall we take my car?' Josh asked extra-politely as hey walked out of the surgery. 'We don't need to take two.'

'Your car is fine,' she said. She wasn't looking forward either to a strained silence between them or an even more strained conversation. But it had to be.

In fact, there was no problem. As soon as he got in the car he turned on the radio and said, 'There's a programme on for the next half-hour about rural development. Apparently they're thinking of funding cottage hospitals again. I'm recording it, but I thought we might listen to it.'

'A good idea,' she said. She didn't say that it would relieve them of the problem of talking to each other.

The programme was interesting, but they arrived at Dark End cottage before it ended and there was already a car outside. Cassie Beynon must be waiting for them.

'I'd like to hear the end of that,' she said without

thinking as the car stopped. 'There are things we ought to think about.'

'I told you I was recording it. I'll be happy to lend you the tape.'

He doesn't sound very happy, she thought.

Dark End cottage was a mess outside. Cal was right, it should be condemned. It was a bigger mess inside. And Barry had obviously deteriorated since the last time he had been examined. Within minutes of meeting him Erin had formed a provisional diagnosis. Barry was not fit to look after himself. And no one was fit to live in this damp-ridden building.

By contrast Cassie Beynon was moving like a tornado. She had already cooked Barry a meal, sorted out future meals and tidied what she could.

She walked over to greet them. Erin noticed that for such an athletic-looking person she had a curiously ungainly walk. A limp almost.

'I'm Cassie Beynon,' she said, offering her hand to Josh and looking at him with approval. 'Barry's social worker. Call me Cassie. And you are Dr…?'

'Dr Josh Harrison. Call me Josh.'

'And I'm Dr Erin Hunter,' Erin said firmly, offering her own hand. 'Call me Erin.'

Cassie was tall, red-haired, an extrovert. She waved her hand at the dilapidated living room. 'A care worker's supposed to keep an eye on this place. I'm going to have a word with her when I get back. It's a disgrace.'

She turned to Barry. 'We'll soon have you sorted out, won't we, Barry?'

Barry beamed vacantly at the three of them, but said nothing.

Cassie put an arm round his shoulders and looked at him with obvious affection. 'We had a long talk before you came, didn't we, Barry?' she said. 'Barry feels that with a bit of help he can look after himself.'

Erin had noticed that Barry had been holding his forearm, rubbing it gently from time to time. Now Josh stepped forward, gently took Barry's arm and rolled up the dirty shirtsleeve. He peeled back an equally dirty bandage. Erin winced. There was an angry weal—a burn, she thought—and it was obviously turning septic.

'How did you do this, Barry?' Josh asked quietly. 'Did you burn yourself on the stove?'

'Burn on the stove,' Barry repeated thoughtfully. He wandered off into the kitchen.

'How about if I take Barry into the bedroom and examine him?' Josh suggested. 'And I'll put a clean dressing on that arm. Meanwhile, Erin, you talk to Cassie about finding somewhere for Barry to move to.'

'Now, just a minute,' Cassie said. 'I'm not sure I agree with this. Barry is happy here, he's lived here all his life. He can manage. Moving him would be terrible. I guess the care worker here hasn't been doing too good a job. I'll make sure she does better in future. But we can't just move a man because he's slowing down a bit.'

She stopped a minute and then said forlornly, 'And I just don't know where I could put him.'

'I'll examine him,' Josh said, 'then if you like Dr Hunter will examine him, too. We'll give you our diagnosis. I'm sorry about your difficulties, I really am, but we must do our job.'

'Perhaps he wants to live here until he dies!' Cassie snapped.

'Perhaps he does. But I'm not going to be responsible for his death.'

It was obvious that Cassie already thought she knew what their verdict would be, and Erin suspected she was right. Neither she nor Josh would find Barry fit to look after himself. But they would conduct a proper examination.

'Just six weeks,' Cassie wheedled. 'Things will be easier then, I'll be able to fit him in with no trouble. He's managed all right for long enough. What's another six weeks?'

'No family?' Erin asked. 'No close friends? No one who could move in with him for a few weeks?'

'Neither family nor friends. Don't worry, I've checked.'

'I'll get on with my examination,' Josh said.

They both examined him. Physically, Barry was malnourished and had a number of uncared-for cuts and scratches on his body. Then there were a number of simple questions they had to ask him. Who was the Prime Minster? What month was it? Could he do the simplest of mental arithmetic? Could he remember a number for five minutes? Barry failed. He would have to leave his home, and be looked after in an institution. Cassie accepted the verdict with as much grace as she could and after the necessary paperwork was completed, Josh and Erin left.

Erin felt a little more relaxed now she had worked with Josh. It had pulled them together. 'Cassie felt we were being a bit hard,' she said as they drove down the tiny road leading from the cottage. 'She felt that since Barry had managed somehow so far we should have allowed her a bit of leeway.'

'Once a doctor starts trying to make other people's lives easier by altering what he knows is best for the patient, then he's in deep trouble. I did sympathise with Cassie and I didn't want to make her life harder. But I'm not going to endanger a patient just to be nice to her.'

'You've got a very direct view of morality. Are all your decisions so easy to make?'

'Not all my decisions,' he said after a while. 'But medical ones tend to be clear cut.'

'I see. The case reported last week—a surgeon refusing to perform a lung transplant because the patient said he wouldn't give up smoking, wouldn't try to lose weight.'

'The surgeon in question had a waiting list of about four months. He didn't take the afternoon off, he performed the operation on someone more deserving.'

Erin pounced. 'Deserving? A doctor only treats those who are deserving?'

Josh laughed. 'You've got me there. Sorry, I must retreat and say—' His mobile phone rang.

'We're just turning onto the main road, about a mile from Dark End Cottage... Yes, we could turn round, we've got no other calls... I know it, it's only five minutes away... We'll let you know at once.'

He slowed, then pulled the car round with a squeal of tyres. 'There's been an accident at the Hayden quarry, it's about three miles down the road. Ambulance is on its way but they want us to lend a hand in the meantime.'

Erin nodded. This wasn't an unusual request. Ambulances could take quite some time to arrive in this widespread country area.

'What kind of accident?' she asked.

'Some mechanical fault at the top of one of those rock-crushing machines. Two men caught, both crushed by rocks. The staff has been told not to try to move them.'

'Good,' Erin said faintly. 'Did you say the top of the machine? We'll have to climb up?'

'I'm sure there'll be steps,' Josh said.

CHAPTER FIVE

IF THERE had been time, Erin would have worried. But almost at once they were turning through great gates marked HAYDEN QUARRY, passing monstrous lorries loaded with sand and gravel. They came to a gatehouse, where Josh leaned out and said they were doctors. The gatekeeper pulled up the barrier and pointed them across the flat quarry floor.

'Glad you got here so quickly. That hopper there, you'll see the men waving to you. When the ambulance comes I'll send it after you. Just a minute.'

He went back into his little cabin and reappeared with two hard hats. 'All visitors have to wear these. Regulations.'

The quarry was vast. A great lunar-like landscape with manmade cliffs and weird machines pressed against them. Everything was covered by a grey dust, which rose and eddied behind them as they drove across the flat floor to where they could now see a man waving.

From a distance the size of the rock-crushing machine hadn't been apparent, but when they pulled up just underneath it Erin could see it was huge. She got out of the car and looked upwards to where, impossibly high, a group of men clustered on a platform. Sets of steps, open to the world, ran up to it. She shivered in horror.

A man in dusty overalls ran over to them. 'Doctors? Thank God you've come. We just don't know what to do. These men need more than first aid. It was terrible. It just shouldn't have happened but—'

Josh opened the boot of the car. 'Can you get some of your men to carry these two bags up for us? And tell me what happened—and how long ago?'

'Eddie, Mac, get these two cases up there!' The man pointed upwards. 'It happened about ten minutes ago. You see, we feed rocks into that hopper, they drop downwards and they're crushed into smaller pieces. Well, one of the metal sides of the hopper gave way, the rocks poured out and some of them fell on a couple of maintenance men.'

Erin winced. This could be messy.

The man went on, 'We've stopped the crusher, of course, things are quite safe now. And we've pulled the stones off the men, tried to stop what bleeding we can.'

'Have you moved them at all?' Josh's voice was sharp.

The man shook his head. 'Not at all. We've been told in lectures to wait until somebody qualified says they can be moved.'

'Good. Now, I'm Dr Harrison and this is Dr Hunter. All we're going to do is look at your men, patch them up a bit and wait for the ambulance.' Josh glanced upwards. 'Getting injured men down from there is going to take specialised equipment, stretchers they can be fastened into. We won't try to move them.'

'Whatever you say. You're in charge now, we'll do whatever you think fit.' Obviously the man had been shocked by the accident.

Erin had listened to what was being said but had let Josh take charge, do the organising. She kept her eyes fixed on the quarry floor, not wanting to look upwards at what seemed the impossible heights above her. She felt sick, terrified.

Josh must have turned to look at her. 'Erin? Are you OK? You look a bit white.'

It was a while before she could reply, and when she did her voice sounded choked. 'I'm…I'm…not very good at heights.'

She knew she was swaying and closed her eyes. Half-memories came flooding back, of sliding, tumbling down an ice slope, of a free fall that had lasted just long enough for her to wonder if she was going to die, and then a split second of agony before there had been merciful blackness. For months it had been a nightmare she suffered once or twice a week. Now it was less often—but it still hadn't disappeared.

She opened her eyes to see him looking at her thoughtfully. His voice was surprisingly sympathetic as he said, 'There's no problem. The paramedics will be here soon with the ambulance. I can manage quite well without you.'

From somewhere she found the courage. 'Two people injured, two doctors are better. I'm going with you. Now, can we get started?'

If she needed to climb those dreadful stairs then she needed to start before what little courage she had leaked away.

'Want me to follow you? Keep close behind?'

'No! You go first. But don't…don't go too fast.' With a grim effort to hang onto her dignity she said, 'We don't want to have another accident, do we?'

She managed by not looking down or to the side, by keeping her gaze fixed on Josh's legs as he climbed steadily in front of her. A distant, detached part of her mind registered that his smart clothes were getting covered in dust, and she wondered how bedraggled her own dress and shoes were looking.

When she was nearly at the top she caught a glimpse of the ground so far below, and she swayed again and felt sick. But she kept moving.

Finally they reached the platform where the two men lay. There were worried-looking workmates around them, who moved back as soon as Erin and Josh arrived.

Erin knelt by the first man. Now she could concentrate on her work, and a little of her fear left her. She opened the first bag, snapped on a pair of rubber gloves.

The two injured men had been made as comfortable as possible, blankets wrapped round them and under their heads. The man Erin had chosen was unconscious. Almost automatically she did the ABC check—airways, breathing, circulation. No problem there. Next, she reached for a hard collar and, carefully supporting the head, fixed it on. It might not be necessary but why take the chance?

There was a long gash across the man's shoulder leading down towards his chest. And it had bled. The blanket was sodden with blood, possibly an artery had been nicked. One of the workmen was very properly pushing a pad down over the wound. When he made to move Erin stopped him. She lifted the pad for a second, then told him to hold it down firmly again.

Just time for a very quick examination of the rest of the body. One leg was grossly deformed below the knee, obviously badly fractured. There was little she could do about it now but it meant that almost certainly there would be blood leaking into the tissues.

The second bag that had been carried up held the emergency equipment. Erin reached into it and took out a giving set. The man needed a plasma expander, otherwise he could go into shock and die. Erin cleaned the inside of an arm, found a vein and slid in the cannula.

Then she connected the bottle and hung it from its stand. It was an emergency measure, but it would keep the man alive until the hospital could cross-match his blood and transfuse that into him.

There was no way she could deal with the gash on the man's chest. It would need a surgeon in Theatre to clean it properly and suture it. She did the best she could, cleaning a little, sprinkling on antiseptic and finishing with a temporary dressing. It would do for the time being. Then she checked the rest of the body for obvious trauma, and found none.

Now she turned to see how Josh was coping, to see if there was anything she could do to help. Josh's patient was half-conscious. He was mumbling, 'I can't feel my legs, Doctor. I'm going to be all right, aren't I?'

She noticed that Josh didn't say yes, just that the man should try to keep still, that he would be treated properly in hospital.

This man, too, had odd abrasions and cuts. Josh had dressed them. He had put a hard collar on the man. But that was all.

She looked at Josh, lifting her eyebrows. He shrugged. There was nothing more that could be done here, the man needed the facilities of a hospital.

Erin took a notebook from the bag. 'Who was here first?' she asked. 'Who helped take the rocks off these two men?'

Three men had done that. First Erin took the names of the two injured men, then she took detailed notes as to where the rocks had fallen on them. It might help the hospital.

Something had been registering in a corner of her mind, now it became more real. It was the sound of an ambulance siren. She didn't look up, didn't wonder what was happening, but soon there was the clatter of feet on the iron steps and two green-clad paramedics came to kneel by her and Josh.

'We're going to need to strap them tight to get them down these steps,' one said.

'I can help,' Josh said. 'I've been on a course in mountain rescue, and part of it was how to secure people in stretchers. I think we need to move this man first.'

This wasn't Erin's area of expertise. She kept to one side as the three men placed their hands under Josh's patient, gently moved him onto the stretcher and then fastened the straps that would hold him still. There was no shortage of volunteers to carry the man down. Erin remained with her own patient, looking only at him.

Five minutes later the paramedics were back with another stretcher. She let them take her unconscious patient and then made sure they had the notes she had made for the doctors in A and E.

And then she, Josh and a couple of workmen were alone on the platform. 'We'll take your bags down,' one of the workmen said gruffly. And she and Josh were alone. Now she had to get back down. It would be worse than coming up.

He appeared to recognise her fear. 'Would you like to hold my hand as we climb down?' he asked.

She thought there was sympathy in his voice but she still had to be strong. 'I'm all right, thanks. I don't need help in going down.'

'Everyone needs help sometimes,' he said. 'Here, take it. Pretend it's for my sake, not yours.'

So she took his hand, though she hated herself for holding it so tightly, and for letting him feel the tremors of fear.

'Have you always suffered from vertigo?' he asked when they finally reached the ground.

'No. And I'd be pleased if you didn't tell anyone at the surgery about it.'

'As you wish. When did you—?'

'And I don't want to talk about it either,' she said. 'Not in any way, not at all.'

'Once again, as you wish. Though people say that it helps.'

'Thank you, but I'm not looking for help. Now, the ambulance has gone so we'd better say goodbye to the foreman here and be on our way.' Erin looked downwards. 'I look a mess.'

'We both do.' Josh thought for a minute and then said, 'You can never tell, of course, but I suspect that if you hadn't given that man the plasma expander, he might well have died. You saved his life, Erin.'

'It's possible,' she said after a while. 'You would have done the same.'

'True. But you did it, and it cost you a lot to climb those steps. How d'you feel about it?'

'It's just my job.'

She knew her voice was curt, knew also that he was reaching out to her. But there seemed little she could do.

There was still some tension between them but they had been thrown together in a difficult and possibly dangerous situation so it was inevitable that they should feel a little more at ease with each other. They talked, about inconsequential medical things. Each was wary, but things weren't as fragile as they had been before. Then her mobile rang.

To her surprise and pleasure it was Jeremy. She had talked to him on the phone two or three times, but usually he rang her when he knew she wouldn't be at work.

'Jeremy, so good to hear from you!'

'Good to speak to you. Are you being kept busy up there?'

'Very busy.' She thought of telling him exactly what she had just been doing, but decided not to. A quick glance at Josh's set face suggested that it wouldn't be a good idea. 'Is this just a social call or have you something specific in mind?'

'You guessed. It's something specific. I've been offered a year's placement in a very good hospital in America—in Boston, as it happens. And I can take a junior colleague with me to help with my research. The money will be good, the training excellent. How would you like to come with me?'

'Come with you? To America?'

'Certainly.'

'I can't just give up everything and come with you to America!'

'You wouldn't be giving up everything. And you'd be back after a year. This is a fantastic career opportunity for you, Erin.'

'When would you be going?'

'Probably in about five months. Could you cut down your stay in the Lakes to six months instead of a year?'

Well, yes, she probably could. But… 'This is a bit of a shock, Jeremy. I've got my life mapped out, I know what I'm doing next. Well, I thought I knew.'

'I'm sure it is a shock. I don't want an answer now, you need time to consider. I'll send you some details and you can think about it. I really would like you to come with me, Erin.'

'And I'd be… I do need time to think, Jeremy, you're right.'

'Good to talk to you. Bye!'

She clicked off her mobile and stared out of the window.

'Good news?' Josh asked after a while. His voice was cold.

'Possibly. My friend Jeremy has offered me a post in America for a year. I'd learn a lot there.'

'With Jeremy. Why did he pick you, I wonder? Was it your medical and academic qualities? Or your personal ones?'

She knew what he meant at once. Anger lanced through her but she managed to keep calm. 'Jeremy knows enough about my work to trust me to be able to do the job. What personal interest there is is that of a friend, it's certainly not anything more. He wouldn't offer me a job if he didn't think I could do it.'

'I'm sure he wouldn't,' Josh said sardonically, and that angered her even more.

'I forgot, you're an expert on women who better themselves by going to America. Have you ever thought that your precious Annabelle might have deserved the promotion she got when she left you? Or have you ever thought that the older, senior man she was seeing might have been able to offer her something that you couldn't? Something like love, or trust, or belief?'

There was silence in the car. She couldn't turn to look at him, the very thought of his expression frightened her. After a moment she muttered, 'I'm sorry, I shouldn't have said that. It was cruel and unnecessary. I know nothing about your affairs.'

Josh didn't reply at first. The silence lengthened, and she started to wonder how she would ever be able to work with this man if he refused to speak to her. Then he said evenly, 'There's no need to apologise. I was equally unpleasant to you.'

'Dishonours equal,' she said.

After a while he said, 'We were getting on so well, Erin. I thought…that perhaps I might…we might…'

'Things change,' she said. She desperately wanted to confide in him, but she just couldn't do it.

She had some time to spare the following night—a Thursday—so she went to a meeting of the amateur dramatic society in the village hall. She'd see Miss Cole there and for too long she had been in the rather intense atmosphere of the surgery. It would be good for her to have a change.

She walked into the village hall and found the group sitting in a circle, notebooks and scripts clutched in their laps. Miss Cole stood and welcomed her. She was not noticeably hampered by her Zimmer frame. 'This is Dr Erin Hunter, who used to be in my school dramatic club. She was one of the most gifted young players I ever taught. I'm sure she'll be an asset to the group.'

Cautiously Erin said, 'It's good to be here and I'd like to help. But I won't be able to come regularly, work will get in the way.'

'I'll see that it doesn't,' a voice said, and everyone laughed. Erin blinked. Then she realised that one of those sitting in the circle was Eunice, the practice manager.

'What are you doing here, Eunice?'

'I'm an amateur actress,' Eunice said placidly. 'I've been a member here for years. You don't think that the practice is my entire life, do you?'

'We're trying to decide on a scene or a play to enter for the Cumbria One Act Play Competition,' Miss Cole said with some irritation. 'And as usual we can't make up our minds. Last year we came third. This year we want to win.'

Erin had forgotten the atmosphere of amateur dramatics. Now she remembered the almost feverish excitement she used to feel when her group—led by Miss Cole—was choosing a play, deciding on sets, rehearsing, finally performing. She remembered the petty jealousies, the unlikely friendships, the pointless arguments. And most of all she remembered how clannish they were. At school she had mixed almost exclusively with the drama group. Her friends had been limited.

Erin remembered the Cumbria competition. Her school had entered the junior section and had won once and come second twice. But this was to be the senior section, and the members were just as anxious to win as she had been all those years before.

The group talked about various options and eventually decided that they would perform a scene out of *The Importance of Being Earnest*. Miss Cole's suggestion. Miss Cole then felt that enough decisions had been made, they would have a cup of tea and then read a play. Erin tried not to let her smile show. Her old teacher must be in her late sixties, but she still knew what she wanted and still intended to have her own way. The little group could not stand up to her.

Erin was drinking her tea and having a quiet word with Eunice when Miss Cole came up to her and gave her an opened script. 'We're going to read a bit of *A Streetcar Named Desire*,' she said. 'I've picked this scene here. You're to play Blanche. Look through it while you drink your tea.'

Erin gulped. 'I can't do this! Blanche's the main part. You must have someone else who—'

'Our usual female lead isn't here. Blanche is a young, tormented woman. You are the perfect choice.'

'But I haven't done anything like this in years! I can't act any more, I'm just a dull—'

'For goodness' sake, Erin Hunter! I'm asking you to read for ten minutes. If you can't act then it doesn't matter, there are those here who can. Or think they can.'

Miss Cole's voice dropped for the last few words, and Erin had to smile. This was the woman she remembered.

'Just do your best,' Miss Cole said.

'I'll do what I can.' But she was dreading it. Acting was a kind of self-revelation and she didn't want to reveal anything of herself. She wanted her feelings to be hidden.

'You'll be good at it, Erin,' Eunice said gently. 'And we're a kind bunch of people anyway. No one will judge you.'

'It's just a bit of a shock, that's all,' Erin said. 'I came here intending to make the tea or pull the curtain.'

'Most of us started that way. Now, read the passage and I'm sure you'll be great.'

Erin skimmed through the excerpt Miss Cole had marked and blinked again. The play was set in the southern states of America, her part that of a woman tortured by her past and by self-doubts. Vaguely she remembered seeing the film—starring Marlon Brando and Vivien Leigh?

She read it through a second time, more closely. It was a brilliant scene in a brilliant play, and after a couple of minutes she found herself muttering her lines. She could feel Blanche, knew and understood her agony, her indecision, her longing for some kind of certainty. It would be important not to reveal too much early in the scene, the final climax must come as a shock to the

audience. She wouldn't bother trying to speak in a southern accent, that would only be comic. And this play was
universal.

'Right, let's make a start,' Miss Cole said. 'Readers
sit here at the front, please.'

'I think I'll just fetch myself a glass of water,' Erin
said. She never used to be nervous. When she was seventeen or eighteen she could have faced this little audience with complete confidence and given a performance
that would have electrified them. Now she was terrified.

Then she remembered. She had come here to lay
ghosts, to try and recover some of the self-assurance she
used to have. Working in Keldale was a test for her.
This must be part of that test.

But even after drinking her water her throat was dry
and she was sure that she wouldn't be able to say a word.

The other three actors taking part in the scene were
quite good, she could appreciate that. By contrast she
hesitated, mumbled her lines, had to repeat herself. She
was terrible! But no one said anything. The faces watching her were interested, sympathetic, alert.

And slowly she eased her way into the part. She felt
for Blanche, she was Blanche, Blanche's pain was hers.
Her voice rose and fell, not as she wished it to but as
the lines demanded. And when she reached the final
screaming, sobbing climax, she felt real tears running
down her face.

She looked up. Her little audience weren't now just
mildly sympathetic, now they were stunned. There was
silence for a moment and then the entire group clapped.

'Very good, all of you,' said Miss Cole.

The meeting ended shortly afterwards, Erin promising
that she would come as often as her work would permit.
Miss Cole had been given a lift to the meeting by a

friend, and as he went to fetch his car Erin had a word with her old teacher in the porch.

'Why did you pick that scene for us to read?' she asked.

'I picked it for *you* to read,' came the robust reply. 'I always said that drama was therapeutic. Now I've just seen it proven.'

'Who's in need of therapy?' Erin asked rather angrily. 'I certainly am not.'

'You certainly aren't the girl I knew nine years ago,' Miss Cole said tartly, 'and, quite frankly, that was the girl I preferred. See you next week, Erin.'

A car drew up in front of the hall and she hopped nimbly down the steps to it.

'A star was born last night,' Eunice said cheerfully. 'We heard Erin read at the drama group, she was brilliant.'

It was the next morning. Cal had called the senior staff together for a quick meeting to discuss new proposals for government funding. Now they were drinking coffee together and having a general chat. He looked up with interest. 'You've started acting again, Erin? That's great.'

She shook her head, embarrassed by Eunice's compliment and Cal's interest.

'Not at all. I just called in last night because...because my old drama teacher asked me to. I don't intend to take an active part. I'm too busy here for a start.'

'We don't mind going to a bit of trouble to make things easier for you to attend meetings,' Cal said. 'Eunice has been telling me about this competition for months.'

'I don't mind filling in for Erin,' Josh said unexpectedly. 'I'll be happy to swap duties with her if she wishes.'

'No, please,' said Erin. 'I just don't want that. First of all, I don't need any favours, I'm here to do a job. Secondly…I'm not sure I want to act any more. I don't think I'm any good at it.'

'That's not what everyone thought last night,' Eunice said. 'If you were our lead, we'd win the competition, that's certain.'

'We're not pushing you, Erin,' Cal said amiably. 'Well, I'm not even if Eunice is. Just let us know if there's anything we can do. Now, is there any more business…?'

Josh was sitting next to her. She didn't think this had been a matter of choice. He had come late to the meeting and there had only been two available seats left. Now he said quietly to her, 'I didn't know you were taking up acting again.'

'Acting is just pretending,' she said bitterly. 'I'm good at that.'

That afternoon she went out on her rounds with Lyn again, visiting new mums and babies. Cal believed that his trainees should spend some time with the midwife, the district nurse and the health visitor so that they understood the work of the other professionals in the practice. In fact, Erin very much enjoyed going out with Lyn. This wasn't illness, this was health. There was something satisfying about seeing so many perfect new babies, so many pleased new mums, even though there were some problems.

'How're you getting on in the cottage?' Lyn asked. 'Are you comfortable there?'

'It's wonderful,' Erin answered. 'I felt at home the

minute I walked in, and I couldn't think of anywhere better to live.'

'You're getting on with your neighbour? You and Josh rubbing along all right?'

Was there something just a little too casual in Lyn's question? If there was a hint there, Erin would ignore it.

'We're getting on fine. We don't live in each other's pockets, though. I see more of him in the surgery than I do at home.'

'I see. You know that Adam claims that the cottage is haunted? Not afraid of ghosts, are you?'

'No. I worry more about the living than the dead. Who is it that's supposed to haunt the place?'

Lyn giggled. 'Adam says that it's a woman who had fifteen children there. She was so happy that she makes everyone who lives in the cottage fall in love. We fell in love there. I think Cal and Jane did the same.'

'That's not going to happen to me,' Erin said with conviction. 'There's no chance at all.'

'That's what I thought. I was wrong. But perhaps you'll be different.'

I'm certainly different, Erin thought.

Josh had slipped into the practice general office for a quick word with Eunice. There were some prescription details that he had to attend to and she had asked him to sign a couple of forms for his bank. The practice seemed to generate an enormous amount of paperwork. Eunice left the patients' notes to the doctors and dealt with all the rest herself. All the staff were tremendously grateful to her.

'I haven't seen Erin this afternoon,' Josh said casually when their business was concluded. 'Is she out with someone?'

'Doing the rounds with Lyn. Did you want her for something?'

'Nothing that can't wait.' Josh lifted a pile of papers from Eunice's desk, casually straightened then and replaced them exactly where they had been before. 'I was interested to hear that she'd been acting again. You know I was at school at the same time as her? I saw her act in the school plays. She was good.'

'She's more than good now, she's fantastic. Last night she played Blanche—you know, out of *A Streetcar Named Desire*. I've never seen a better performance of a woman tormented by doubt and guilt and despair. She wasn't acting, she was living it.'

'Was she?' Josh asked thoughtfully. 'Tormented by doubt and guilt and despair? That's a lot to carry.'

He had a full afternoon, seeing patients, and as usual enjoyed himself. He knew he was gaining experience, learning how to read his patients, how to assess them in the few minutes he had with them. He now knew that being a GP meant far more than dealing with the illnesses or complaints that people brought him. So often the apparent complaints covered a deeper need.

His last patient took far too much of his allocated time, but Josh thought it was worth it. He persuaded George Grimley, a sixty-two-year-old farmworker, to go to hospital and have tests on his prostate. For months now—according to his case notes—George had been resisting pressure to go for further examination. Now Josh had convinced him, and he was slightly pleased with himself.

Now it was five o'clock. He would go home, have a snack and relax a while before coming back for his evening session. The receptionists were about to leave, the surgery would be shut now for a couple of hours. He was the last doctor in the building—no, there was Erin coming down from the library, a couple of books under her arm. She gave him a strained smile and he wondered...

There was the clatter of feet down the corridor and they both looked up as a young man, by his clothes a farmworker, rushed into Reception. 'Please, is there a doctor here? We need to see a doctor, we need him fast! It's my dad, I've got him in the car.'

Josh and Erin exchanged glances. Josh shrugged. The practice wasn't equipped for emergencies, but it was some distance to the nearest hospital and it wasn't unusual for them to have to cope as best they could.

'We'll come and have a look,' Josh said. 'But we might have to send him to the hospital A and E.'

Right by the surgery front door, its engine still running, was an ancient car that by the filth on it looked as if it was usually parked in the middle of a farmyard. The lad ran in front of them and opened the back door. Erin looked in just after Josh and heard his sigh of dismay. There was a man lying across the back seat, an older man also dressed in farmworkers' clothes. His face was contorted in pain and his hands clutched a dirty towel to his leg. Blood dripped and spilled from under the towel onto the car floor. And the man smelt. Erin saw the green-grey stains over his clothes and realised that he had been immersed in fresh farmyard manure.

'He was in the yard at the back of the tractor,' the lad sobbed. 'We had this wire trace round the towing ball and it got caught in his leg. I drove off and dragged him halfway across the yard before I heard him yelling. Is he going to be all right?'

Josh turned to her. 'We can't send him to hospital like this.'

'Certainly not yet,' she agreed. 'We'll have to clean him up a bit, try to stop some of that bleeding. Is there anyone else here?'

'Just us two doctors and the receptionists. D'you feel we can cope?'

'Of course we can cope,' she said coolly. 'Let's face it, we have to.'

One of the receptionists had followed them down the corridor and Josh sent her back to fetch out a wheeled stretcher. Then he went to the other side of the car and got into the back seat behind the injured man's head.

'We're going to have to lift you out,' Erin heard him say gently. 'It might hurt a bit as we move you, but it'll be soon over. Who are you, by the way?'

'Name's Allan Farrow. Lallans Farm.'

'Right, Allan. I'll support your head and your son and the other doctor will take your legs. Ready?'

Erin took the injured leg and held the weight as the three of them gently levered Allan out of the car and onto a stretcher. Then she lifted the towel from the man's leg and winced. It was bleeding and it was filthy. It was going to take some cleaning up.

The weather was warm, she'd been wearing a light blue summer dress, almost sleeveless. It was an attractive dress, and had been expensive. As she straightened she saw that much of the dirt and blood on Allan had transferred itself to her. Well, perhaps the dress would wash.

They wheeled Allan into the treatment room and sent the son to sit in the waiting room. 'We don't need two doctors,' she said. 'We need a doctor and a nurse. And this time I'm volunteering to be the nurse. How about if I get Allan cleaned up as much as I can, then you can treat him?'

He looked at her thoughtfully. 'That's a good idea,' he said. 'I'll go and scrub up, you do what you can.'

She found an apron but she knew it wouldn't give her too much protection. Well, get on with the job. First she had to cut the clothing away from the injured leg. It wasn't quite as bad as they had feared at first. There were several deep cuts and considerable abrasion, but not enough to need skin grafts. She laid temporary pads over the worst of the cuts and concentrated on washing as much of the dirt away as she could.

She knew Josh was now watching her. 'Don't try to help me,' she said. 'You need to stay sterile.'

'Fair enough. I'd really like all the clothes off him. We need to examine all of his body.'

'I'll see to it.'

Another dirty job but she knew it was necessary. As she worked she talked to Allan—she knew that for anyone in pain, a comforting friendly voice was a great relief.

'You are in a mess, Allan. But don't worry, your leg isn't as bad as we thought. It's a good thing your son was with you, he's done a great job getting you here…'

Finally she thought he was ready. She stepped back, waved Josh forward. And there behind Josh was Cal.

'Cal, I didn't hear you come in!'

'I was in the house at the back, the receptionist called me because it was an emergency.' Cal looked at Josh. 'This is now your case, you carry on. Both of you carry on. I'll just stand here and watch. Anything you want me to do?'

'Phone for an ambulance,' said Erin. 'I know it might take some time but we can only do so much here.'

'I agree,' said Josh. 'He needs X-raying for a start.'

Josh treated the worst of the cuts and put on temporary

dressings, having given Allan a pain-killing injection. Then he carefully inspected the rest of the body for further injuries. Cal looked on and said nothing. Erin offered her opinion when she was asked for it. Finally the ambulance came and took Allan away. His son couldn't go with him as he had to go back to the farm for the milking.

'A job well done, I think,' said Cal. 'The decision to have one of you as the cleaner and one as the more-or-less sterile doctor was a good one.'

'That was Erin's idea,' Josh said. 'She volunteered.'

Cal turned to Erin and grinned. 'I've never seen you look so dirty or smell so badly,' he said. 'Somehow you've even got cow muck in your hair. D'you want to go home and change?'

Erin took off the apron and looked down at her now ruined dress. 'I'd hoped to wear this another day,' she said. 'Well, I've got more at home.'

'Once again, you both did a great job there,' Cal said. 'But I still want you back for evening surgery. Want a lift back, either of you?'

'I'll walk. I wouldn't want to mess up your car,' Erin said.

As usual there were forms and reports to fill in. Josh volunteered to do them. But before he started he looked out of the window at Erin's disappearing figure. He thought about what he had just seen her do. Cleaning up Allan had been an unpleasant job and she had done it— happily, willingly, without showing any distaste whatsoever.

The two situations were completely different, but would a woman like that reject a man she loved because he had had part of a leg amputated? Somehow Josh didn't think so.

So what exactly had happened? He was beginning to think that he had judged Erin far too quickly.

He couldn't tell her, but every time he saw her his heart lurched. She looked both gorgeous and vulnerable. Perhaps he could have helped her. Would he now ever get the chance?

CHAPTER SIX

'CALL yourself a doctor, call this a surgery! You know nothing!'

The woman stood at the door of Erin's room, white-faced, almost incoherent with rage. 'I'm a respectable woman, I've got a husband and children and a house. I won't come here again!'

'Mrs Senior, if you could just come and sit down. I'm sorry if—'

'I'll give you sorry! I'll go somewhere else and get a real doctor, not a kid just out of college.' She turned her head and looked down the corridor. 'And you lot, what d'you think you're staring at? You're all the same, I know, you're all the same.'

Then there was the rattle of feet in the corridor and afterwards the growing hum of alarmed conversation. Erin sat there shaking, trying to control the tears that ran down her face.

Cal came into the room. 'Did she touch you?'

Numbly, Erin shook her head.

'Good. Now, sit there, I'll calm things down outside and get someone to take the rest of your patients. Then I'll bring you a coffee and we'll talk about things.'

He was with her in five minutes. 'Take your time,' he said. 'We all have bad or troublesome patients from time to time, it goes with the job. When you're ready, tell me all about it.'

Erin was trembling so much that she needed two

hands to hold her coffee-cup. 'I wanted to help her,' she said. 'She needed help.'

'We can only help those who will co-operate with us. Medicine is a two-way process. Now, try to think coolly about what happened and we'll see if things could have gone a different way.'

'You mean if I could have handled her better?' Erin asked savagely.

'I don't think that at all. I don't think anything till you tell me what happened.' Cal's voice was calming.

She took a deep breath, drank more coffee. Then, in a monotone, she said, 'Janet Senior, she's a visitor. Aged about forty, lives in Birmingham and doesn't quite remember the name of her home GP. She's on a caravan site with her husband—she was vague about exactly where. Told me she'd fallen over a couple of days ago, her back hurt so could I give her some painkillers. I asked to see her back, she said she didn't want to undress, just painkillers would do. Her husband said so. But somehow I managed to get her to lift up the back of her sweater.'

She stopped and thought about what she had seen, what she had said.

'Her husband was waiting outside,' Cal said after a while. 'He was in a hurry to get her away.'

'I wonder why. Well, she did need painkillers. There was a set of cuts and bruises, obviously quite fresh. And I thought there were older ones underneath. I couldn't make sense of it. There were sets of two cuts, about an inch apart and two inches long. Then I remembered a picture I'd seen in a lecture on abuse. The cuts and bruises were made by a belt buckle. Someone had been whipping her with his belt.'

'So you said?'

Erin winced at the memory. 'I asked her who had been whipping her. She said no one so I told her that if she had been abused there was something we could do about it. Was it her husband who…and then she shouted at me and ran out.'

Cal nodded slowly. 'We get cases like this,' he said. 'They're tragic, but there's nothing to be done if the woman won't complain.'

'But I handled her wrong! Didn't I?'

'You used the words "whipping" and "abuse". And you brought her husband into it. Perhaps you should have tried to use less emotive words.'

'Cal, I feel I'm a failure! I've let that woman down. And one thing more. Perhaps she has children.'

'You're tired,' Cal said gently. 'You don't yet know how to take things easy, you put too much energy into things that don't need it. In time you'll learn how to pace yourself, to concentrate on the important things and not worry about the others.'

'It's people,' she said. 'I'm good enough with illnesses and diseases but I'm no good with people. Especially people who shout at me.'

'I don't agree. Now, you haven't got surgery tonight, go home and have a good rest.'

So she went—though she wasn't very happy.

She didn't want to see any more people, she wanted to go straight home to eat, have a bath and go to bed early. As far as she was concerned, the human race could manage without her for a while. She was fed up with people wanting things they couldn't have and blaming her when she wouldn't supply them.

She walked home, went upstairs, wrenched off the dress she'd been wearing and reached for her jeans. Then someone knocked at her front door. Oh, who now?

Her jeans weren't handy so she pulled on her dressing-gown and stamped downstairs. Whoever it was had better get their business over quickly and go!

It was Josh. 'I've brought you a bit of good news and a present,' he said. He offered her a plastic carrier.

'I'm not in the mood for good news and I don't want a present from you.'

He looked at her quizzically. 'I have had more enthusiastic greetings,' he said. 'But we'll let that go. The present isn't from me, it's from Derrick Farrow of Lallans Farm—son of the man we treated yesterday, he called round earlier. The good news is that his dad's going to be all right. The present is a dozen duck's eggs each. And I must say, they look good.'

'Well, thank you,' Erin muttered. 'And I'm sorry if I was rude.'

'That's all right. You've got a problem, I can tell. Want to tell me what it is?'

'No, I don't. Why should I? It doesn't concern you. We work together but we don't much like each other, remember?'

'This isn't a personal problem, it's a work problem, I can tell. So it does concern me. A problem shared is a problem halved. What is it?'

She blinked. She had opened the door to find him on her front step. Now, somehow, they were both in her tiny front hall and he was closing the door behind him.

'Look, I made a mistake this afternoon. Cal had to put it right and I'm wondering if I'm suited to being a GP. Sometimes people just get on top of me.'

'What mistake?'

'I don't want to tell you! You don't make mistakes, you wouldn't understand.'

'I make mistakes,' Josh said soberly. 'I do it regularly.

So tell me what you did and then it'll be a mistake I don't make.'

So she told him and he nodded. 'Easy enough to do,' he said. 'But I can sympathise with how you feel. Someone's screamed at you for doing your job and you don't like it. So what are you going to do? Sit here and feel sorry for yourself?'

'I'm going to do just that! And I'm going to enjoy it all the more because you won't be with me. So would you mind leaving me to it?'

'Yes,' he said. 'I would mind and I'm not going to leave you.'

Her mouth dropped open at this bare-faced cheek.

'You know, when you moved in,' he mused, 'I cooked you spag bol. I told you it was my signature student meal, the one I cooked night after night for comfort when I was studying. You promised to do the same for me some day.'

'I've cooked you a meal,' she pointed out angrily. 'And you said my casserole was a lot more haute cuisine than your spaghetti Bolognese.' Then honesty made her add, 'But I did enjoy your meal.'

'We're not talking about haute cuisine now. We're talking about comfort eating. So cook us your signature meal. You have got one, haven't you? Every medical student I've ever met has got a favourite comfort meal. It's usually something you can make in a bucket in vast quantities and it lasts for days. What's yours?'

'Like I said, we don't like each other, do we? Why do you want to spend time with me?'

'We may not like each other now but something has started between us. And we're certainly attracted to each other.'

'Look what nearly happened last time we were attracted to each other.'

That seemed to worry him, much to her surprise. 'Yes,' he said. 'That is a point. Perhaps I should go.'

Even more to her surprise, Erin found she didn't want him to go. 'Oh, sit down,' she snapped. 'I'll go upstairs and finish getting dressed and then I'll feed you.'

'Thank you. And then we'll talk. We've not been honest with each other, not open enough.'

'I'm not sure that being honest and open is a recipe for a quiet life,' she said as she walked upstairs.

When she came down, more comfortably dressed, and looked in her fridge, her freezer and her cupboards, she found that there was quite a lot of stuff she could use. And there was her wok, she hadn't cooked with that for quite a while. Reluctantly she said, 'I used to do a fried rice dish. It was never the same twice since it was largely made of leftovers, but I liked it.'

'Sounds fantastic. Make a load and freeze the rest. I'll sit quietly here while you rush round and act domesticated.'

'Yes, master,' she muttered, but not loud enough for him to hear.

However, it was calming, working in the kitchen. And it was fun cooking for more than one. She cooked the rice in the microwave oven, found vegetables, fish, a couple of chicken breasts that could all be chopped up small. There was garlic to be fried, and ginger and half a bottle of black bean sauce to be poured in.

It seemed as if she had cooked with lightning speed. Josh disappeared next door and brought back two bottles of red wine. 'Student wine,' he announced. 'For glugging, not sipping.' And then they were sitting opposite each other in her kitchen, an alarmingly large pile of fried rice on each plate.

'This is some meal,' he said. 'May I have the recipe?'

'You may have the lack of a recipe. It all depends on what's left in the cupboard. Once I made it with rice, a tin of baked beans and a tin of pilchards.'

'Every meal an adventure,' he said.

When they had finished Josh insisted on washing up at once and then making coffee. Then they sat in her living room, not side by side but facing each other. 'How d'you feel about the human race now?' he asked.

'I guess I can put up with it. In fact, I guess I'll have to.'

'Right, then we'll talk about just two members of it. Me and you.'

'Do we have to?' Erin asked sullenly. 'Can't you think of anything more fascinating?'

'Yes, we do and, no, I can't.' He paused, and then said curiously, 'When I think of you at school I remember you as being outgoing and friendly. You'd talk to anyone. Now you're more reserved—even frightened of people. What happened to you?'

'People change,' she said.

'Not that much. And, besides, every now and again I can see the old Erin showing through. And your hair. It was long and blonde and you let it flow down your back. I used to…I used to want to touch it.'

Her anger flared. 'I just decided on a new style. It's still long but I keep it tied up. Nothing wrong with that, is there?'

She could almost see him thinking. 'What's the problem with your hair, Erin? I know you might need to keep it up when you're working. But now…why now?'

For a while she sat there, her head bowed. Then she

reached up and pulled out the pins so her hair cascaded downwards. She heard him sigh softly.

'Like that, you're beautiful, Erin,' he said.

But her voice was harsh. 'Come and sit next to me. You said you used to want to stroke my hair. Well, now you can.'

He looked at her thoughtfully. It had not been a welcoming invitation. But he came and sat next to her and ran his hand down the long blonde length of her hair. For just a little while she found it calming, peaceful. But that wasn't the purpose of the exercise.

'That could be nice,' she said. 'But it's not why I asked you to do it. Feel just above my left temple.'

So he did. His face was close to hers, it had to be. And she saw the change in his expression, the intent look changing to a frown. Then there was the calm, put-on expression that indicated that the doctor was surprised, but didn't want to show it and scare the patient.

Carefully he parted her hair to see what was below. His touch was gentle but still she jerked a little when he got close.

'Two scars and signs of stitches,' he said. 'At a guess, one scar the result of an accident, the other scar the result of some kind of operation. What was it, a tumour of some sort?'

His voice was now doctor-distant, he was being kind but detached from her. That was good. She didn't want sympathy.

'You're right, the first scar was the result of an accident. The second was an operation to relieve pressure inside the skull. I also needed a neurological investigation.'

'Was it recent?'

'Two years ago. I had to take a year off work to recuperate. It was then that I met Jeremy. He was in charge of my case. I also had a broken arm and extensive bruising and abrasions, but they were comparatively easy to deal with.'

'I see. You obviously had a nasty bang. Were there neurological complications?'

She had started to tell him but this bit was hard. 'There were neurological complications, but technically my problems were in the mind, not the brain. The hospital insisted that I see a psychiatrist—if only because I was going to be a practising doctor myself.'

She saw the understanding dawn on his face. 'The fall off the cliff,' he said. 'With David King on Striding Edge. When you got engaged.'

'How did you know about that? You've been talking about me behind my back, spying on me! I bet you've even talked to him, haven't you?'

Josh's expression told her all she wanted to know. Somehow she managed to hold back the molten heat of her anger. 'Well, you've had your meal, you've found out what you wanted to know. I'd like you to go now. Perhaps you'd like to phone David to tell him what the doctor has found out about the state of mind of his fiancée!'

Josh's face was white but his voice was calm. 'I'm not going. There are things I want to say, things I need to ask you.'

Now Erin was incandescent with rage. She leaped to her feet, kicking over the coffee-table. Two glasses rolled to the floor. 'I told you to go! Do I have to phone someone to have you thrown out?'

He stood in his turn, picked up the table and the glasses. 'That happened before,' he said. 'When we were better friends.'

Then he took her by the arms and pulled her close to him so their faces were only inches apart. For one wild moment she wondered if he was going to kiss her. Well, she would have none of that caveman kind of behaviour.

But he didn't try to kiss her. He said, 'We've got nowhere over the past few weeks because we haven't talked. And that's a pity because I thought when we first met we were going to be honest with each other. And we were starting to mean quite a lot to each other. Well, you meant a lot to me. Now for just half an hour I'm going to be brutally honest, and you're going to be the same. Then I walk out of that door, and if you don't want me to I'll never walk back in again. Agreed?'

That shook her a little, but only a little.

'Agreed,' she said. 'Now, will you, please, let go of me.'

He did release her, and she sat down. For a moment he looked at her and then went back to the seat opposite her.

'I have been round to see David King. He phoned me the day after we met his mother at the rugby club and asked me to come and see him. Then he asked me to keep quiet about the visit, though I saw no reason why I should.' Josh smiled grimly. 'He tried to trap me. Asked me to examine him, said he'd pay privately. I refused.'

Erin was still angry but now she was also intrigued. 'He wanted you to be his doctor,' she said. 'Patient-doctor confidentiality. You couldn't have talked about him.'

'Clever, wasn't it?' He thought for a moment. 'But I didn't like turning down a man who asked for help.'

'So what did he want? What did he tell you?'

'He wanted to know what was my relationship with

you. I told him it was up to you to decide, and he didn't like it.'

'David is always surprised when people don't do what he wants them to,' she said.

Josh nodded. 'I can guess. He also said that the pair of you had always intended to get married. He proposed on the mountainside, you accepted and you wanted to go up Striding Edge to celebrate getting engaged, even though it was dangerous. You both fell. When you found out that he had part of a leg amputated, you wanted nothing more to do with him.'

It was a bald account but she guessed it was an accurate summing-up of the conversation. 'And so you thought I was a pretty low character,' she said. 'You believed that any woman who could reject her fiancé because of an accident that she had caused wasn't worth bothering with?'

'That thought crossed my mind,' he agreed cautiously. 'You know I believe people should stick to what they have promised. And when I tried to ask you about him you got angry and seemed defensive.'

She didn't say anything, just looked at him. After a moment he went on. 'I'm not very pleased with myself. I judged you when I had no right to, no facts to judge you on. I can only say that I was a bit…upset. I'd started to like you quite a lot and you just didn't seem that kind of girl. Yesterday, when I saw you treating that farmer, I knew you'd never turn against a man just because he'd had an amputation. I was confused.'

'So you want my side of the story?' she asked him.

'Very much so. But that's only if you want to tell me.'

'I've got nothing to tell you. Nothing whatsoever.'

The silence between them seemed to stretch on into

infinity. Eventually he said, 'Shall I make us some coffee?'

When he brought the coffee a few minutes later he sat next to her.

'I suppose there is something I can tell you,' she said, pressing her fingers against the side of her head. 'But there's not much. You remember how David and I were at school.'

'Indeed, I do. You were a golden couple.'

'We were both schoolchildren. Anyway, David went to university to study law and I studied medicine. We were just good friends, there was no understanding that I was aware of. We didn't write to each other, we each went out with other people at college. When I came home in the holidays to stay with my parents, we'd go out on the odd date, just for old times' sake really. By this time he'd joined his father's firm of solicitors.'

'Seems straightforward enough,' Josh said.

'That's what I thought. Then just under two years ago he invited me out for a day in the hills. We were going to climb Helvellyn. It was a gorgeous day, but there was snow on the ground and it had frozen.'

She paused, took a breath, tried to keep her voice firm. 'We got halfway up. I remember standing by that little lake, you know, Red Tarn, looking up at the summit. It was gorgeous, but I knew it was dangerous. It was much colder up there than down in the valley, and we had no rope, no ice-axes, no crampons. But we went on anyway, on up Striding Edge.'

She couldn't control the quaver in her voice. 'And that's all I know. Sometimes I get nightmares. I know I'm falling and I'm waiting for the pain. But there was no pain, at least not straight away. I woke up in hospital with a fractured skull, a broken arm and the information that I was lucky to be alive. A mountain rescue team had carried the two of us down the mountain.'

'And you remember…?'

Her voice was flat. 'I remember nothing between standing by the lake and waking up in hospital.'

'Retrospective amnesia,' Josh mused. 'Not unusual after an accident.'

'The consultant couldn't decide whether it was physiological or psychological in origin. Whatever, I just don't remember, though, Lord knows, I've tried.'

'What about the engagement ring?'

'I just can't see myself wanting to get engaged to David! But there again…the fall altered my character. Perhaps I did accept.' She shrugged. 'He wrote to me from hospital enclosing the ring, saying he'd heard that I'd lost my memory, that I'd agreed to marry him and he loved me but we'd have to wait a while till we had both recovered. I was horrified. I wrote back to him to say that I'd lost my memory and that I couldn't make any decisions just then. I sent the ring back. He came to hospital in a wheelchair and there was a dreadful scene in which he accused me of abandoning him because he'd lost his leg. Then his mother came to see me and I agreed to go to see him and there was another dreadful scene. He said it was my fault he lost his leg, that I made him go up Striding Edge.'

'You were under quite some pressure,' Josh said. 'I can sympathise.' His words were calm but comforting, and she was glad he didn't become emotional himself. She was feeling enough emotion for the pair of them.

'Drink your coffee now,' he went on. 'We can finish this later.'

So Erin drank the coffee and she felt better. Telling

the story had eased the pain. Now she was glad that Josh knew. He was right, it was always better to talk.

'So why did you come back here?' he asked after a while. 'Why come somewhere which brings you so many unhappy memories?'

'There are demons I've got to face,' Erin said. 'Ghosts I have to lay. One is David. I've got to get over him, got to lose this feeling of guilt. Sooner or later I'll have to go to see him again, but I've been putting it off. I know he'll still blame me.'

'He does. And don't forget, he's plausible and he's manipulative.'

'Tell me about it. The other thing is, I've got this fear of mountains. I used to do quite a lot of mountain walking, not as much as you perhaps but still quite a lot, and I loved it. And now every time I see something steep, I feel sick.'

'Had it got easier in the weeks you've been here?'

'No,' she said. 'So I'll just serve out my time and go back to London. The third thing is, I've lost all my confidence. I don't deal well with people any more.'

'That'll come back. In fact, it's already doing so. Now, why don't we sit here and be quiet for a while? I think we've had enough emotion for one evening.'

'But we haven't decided anything yet! We've got nowhere.'

'Not at all. I think we've decided quite a lot.'

She looked down. When had he started holding her hand? When had he put his arm round her shoulders? Not that it mattered. She felt warm and comforted and at ease. He was right, there had been quite enough emotion for one night. Perhaps she would shut her eyes for a while.

She wasn't really asleep. But after the emotions of the

past hour, of the past day, in fact, it was comforting just to lie there. He was a comforting man—like a rock. No, rocks were hard. Josh wasn't hard, he was comforting. And also very comfortable.

She leaned towards him and put her arm around his waist. She had been like this with him before. She remembered what had happened, what might have happened if she hadn't hurt his leg. Perhaps doing this again was dangerous. But she liked it so much.

She was a doctor, and doctors listened to heartbeats and so on. You could tell a lot from a heartbeat. Now her hand was over his heart, and through his shirt she could feel his heart beating—fast. 'Why is your heart beating so fast?' she asked.

There was a pause and then he said slowly, 'Because you are exciting me more than is good for me, and I think that perhaps I should go.'

She didn't reply, and the silence between them went on and on. She didn't move. Then, as if from a distance, she heard herself say, 'I don't want you to go.'

He seemed to think about this and asked, 'But do you want me to stay?'

She realised this was a different question. He was asking for a commitment. 'Yes, I want you to stay,' she said after a while.

'I've hated being so distant from you, Erin. Each time I see you there's this great feeling of…of—'

'Is love the word you're looking for?'

There was silence a moment. 'I suppose it could be that,' he said wonderingly.

'Well, I think I feel the same way. But that's enough talking for now.'

For a while there was no movement, she was content to let things take their own slow pace. Then she moved her arm and lay back on the couch, her head on the cushion. She knew it was an invitation.

He kissed her ear. At first she wasn't sure whether it just tickled or whether she liked it, but then she discovered it was sending shudders of pleasure up and down her spine. How strange. The ear was a source of pleasure.

She turned her head to him and closed her eyes, so he kissed them next. Another, strange, distant pleasure. She felt a combination of languor and excitement. For the moment she was happy for him to do to her what he wished. So far he had not even kissed her on the lips.

She felt his hand on her head, lifting her hair, combing it with his fingertips, trailing it down her front. 'So beautiful,' he murmured.

She could feel his uneven breathing, feel the rising of his chest next to her. She guessed what she was doing to him. But she herself felt almost light, as if her body belonged to someone else, as if she could know the pleasure and yet remain detached from it. He hadn't kissed her on the lips yet. And then he did. And with a jolt, all was different.

Before, she hadn't fully realised the strength of her need for him, but she realised it now. And she knew he felt the same way. She could detect an urgency in him that threatened the control he had so far shown.

He was still gentle. But she moaned and pulled him to her, opening her lips and tasting his sweetness, happily accepting his growing passion. Their bodies were pressed together, she could feel his need. They lay there, she didn't know for how long.

But he must be uncomfortable. She was happy, but she was uncomfortable. Sitting side by side on a couch was not the best position for making love. The thought came from nowhere, and she was a little shocked by it. Did she want him to make love to her? She was more shocked by her instant acceptance. Yes, she did want him to make love to her.

She eased him backwards for a moment, looked at that dear face. 'The last time we did this,' she said, her voice unsteady, 'I kicked the table and nearly broke your leg. Come upstairs with me.'

'You mean that?' he asked in a wondering voice. 'Erin, I don't want to hurt you. Are you sure…?'

'You'll hurt me if you don't come,' she said.

She stood, he still looked up at her unbelievingly. Then she stretched out her hand to him and led him to her bedroom.

Quickly she drew the curtains, switched on the bed-side lamp so it shed a soft glow in the room. Then she came over and kissed him. 'I know what I'm doing,' she said. 'I'll prove it to you.' She pointed to her doctor's bag. 'I was out with Lyn last week; we were talking about contraception. There are samples in there. I don't want to get pregnant. You get in bed and I'll go to the bathroom.' She knew she had to move fast.

Erin undressed in the bathroom, leaving her clothes in a heap. First she pulled on her dressing-gown, then she took it off again. She would come to him naked.

Josh was lying in bed, the sheet rolled down to his waist. Quickly she slid under the sheet and threw herself into his arms. She was frightened now, and didn't want time to think.

It was different when both of them were naked. She could feel all of his body, it seemed to match hers so well. Her arms, legs, breasts seemed to fit with him. For a while they were content just to lie side by side and kiss. But then he rolled her onto her back and his lips roamed her body, kissing her as she had never been kissed before.

It felt shameless to let him do it, but it also felt so good.

Then, somehow, when she thought that no greater pleasure was possible, things changed. He was above her, his head a dark shadow, his body poised. For a moment she was afraid. Then she felt for him, urged him gently down onto her, into her. Her sigh of pleasure matched his groan of pleasure. And then it was so much easier.

Neither could wait now. Their joint climax came so swiftly, and she cried aloud in ecstasy. For a while, they lay there.

Then she crept out of bed, opened the curtains and windows and let the breeze cool their sweat-slicked bodies. 'You are so good to me,' she murmured.

Erin woke very early and stared at the ceiling.

In a drawer downstairs she had found a crystal, faceted and cut in the shape of a heart. Lyn had said that it wasn't hers—though Erin wasn't sure whether to believe her. Whatever, Erin had fastened it to her bedroom curtain rail, and now the early morning sun shone through it and cast coloured lights across the ceiling. There was the mildest of breezes coming through the slightly opened window, and it made the crystal twist. The coloured lights danced and she thought they were beautiful.

Gently, she rested a hand on Josh's naked shoulder. He slept on his side, his back to her, and she wanted to move closer to him. She wanted to fit herself to the curve of his spine, to wrap her arm around his waist, to have as much of her body touching his as was possible. But that had been last night. This morning things would have to be different. So she contented herself with the lightest of touches, a hand on his shoulder.

She knew when he was waking. The rhythm of his breathing altered as he came to consciousness. She felt rather sad. Lying beside him had been a tiny, problem-free interlude that she had enjoyed. But now he would wake, and they must talk and decide things.

Then he woke. She knew he was awake as his body tautened and then relaxed again. His hand came up to cover hers, to hold it to his shoulder. She decided they would lie like this for a minute or two longer.

But finally he rolled over, turned to face her. Their eyes were only inches apart. She tried to read what was in his. 'I had a lovely dream,' he said. 'Or was I dreaming?'

'You were dreaming. That was last night, now we have a new day. We forget last night, get on with our lives. As soon as you can creep back next door, that is.'

'You told me once that some things can be forgiven, but never forgotten. And Erin, never, never will I forget last night.'

The passion, the sincerity in his voice was so obvious that she was shocked. But why should she be? She would never forget last night either.

'I'll make you a coffee before you go,' she said. 'You should be able to—'

'You lie here.' He slid out of bed, stood there naked before her. Well, of course, she was a doctor, she had seen many naked males before. But most of them had been ill, or in some surroundings that reduced them to mere anatomical specimens. This was a naked man standing in her bedroom.

She tried to pretend he wasn't there, then something

forced her to look at him. Powerful chest and shoulders, a trim waist, muscular arms and legs. And the…and the…rest of him. Trying to be detached, she said, 'You obviously keep fit.'

'Is that exactly what you were thinking? How strange.' His voice sounded amused. Before she knew what he was doing he had pulled back the sheet that was covering her, bent forward and kissed her. Quickly kissed her breasts, her belly, her…

'Josh, what are you doing?' She grabbed the sheet, dragged it back over her.

'I'm sure you know what I'm doing. The question is, do you like it?'

'That is not the question at all.' She tried to inject some dignity into her voice. 'The question is…the question is…'

'While you think of the question, I'll go to make us both some coffee. Just one condition. You don't get up, don't get dressed, don't put on a nightdress. OK?'

'But I ought to—'

'If you don't agree then I'm getting straight back into bed with you.'

'All right, I agree. I'll stay as I am. But don't think that commits me to anything.'

'I wouldn't dream of thinking any such thing.'

In fact, she did get up quickly to pull a comb through her hair and rub cream on her face. But she was back in bed again when he returned, sitting upright and with the sheet pulled up round her chin.

He was still naked. 'Don't you feel the need to put on any clothes?' she asked.

'It's not cold and I feel comfortable like this. Perhaps I feel welcome, too.'

'Don't bet on it,' she told him.

He had brought up a tray, which balanced on her knee as he slid back beside her. He'd only been downstairs for ten minutes but he'd prepared a tiny feast. There was a pot of coffee, two bowls of fresh fruit salad and whole-grain toast. 'A bit more than the mug of coffee I expected,' she said.

'You need to keep your strength up. We doctors work hard.'

So she ate and drank with him and she enjoyed it. Finally he put the tray on the floor at the side of the bed. She looked at her bedside clock. It was still early.

'Now we talk,' she said.

'I suppose so. But don't you think that actions speak louder than words?'

'I think we've acted enough. Josh, last night was wonderful and, like you, I'll never forget it. But where does it get us?'

'It doesn't need to get us anywhere, it was something marvellous in itself. For a while we were both ecstatically happy, we were lost in each other.'

'That was then, this is now. How do we work together, what do we say when we see each other? Do we just pretend it didn't happen? Don't we wonder if it might happen again?'

He sighed. 'I suppose you're right. We have to make sense of what we're doing.'

'Not too long ago I met you downstairs for the first time in nine years. There was this something between us that grew, almost in spite of us.'

'Yes,' he said. 'It's grown. And now I love you.'

'Perhaps you do. And I think I love you back.' She brooded for a minute and then said, 'Perhaps it would be better if we thought of this as just an unhappy accident and gave each other up. I can see nothing but heartache in it for both of us. And you seem to have suffered enough. So, for that matter, have I.'

He reached over a finger, traced it down the side of her face, onto her neck and shoulder, down the inside of her arm and to the centre of the palm of one hand. It was a slow, gentle caress and it meant more to her than he could have guessed.

He said, 'We're sitting here, stark naked, and talking like an ice man and an ice woman. We're talking about *us*. How did we get this way?'

Erin giggled. 'Perhaps it's not our fault. Lyn told me that this place is haunted. There's a ghost here that makes couples fall in love. It happened with her and Adam, it happened with Cal and Jane.'

'Then it's not fair to put young unmarried doctors in here. Perhaps I'll complain to the BMA. Now, you're evading the question. What do you want?'

She had forgotten Josh's determination, his almost ruthless passion for getting things right. Slowly, she said, 'I came up here to lay ghosts. I need closure with David. I need to get over my great horror of mountains. It's silly. And I need my confidence back. And until I get those things, or at least some of them, I'll never be able to have a wholehearted relationship. Josh, I'm only half a woman.'

She had wondered if he would understand, but apparently he did. 'I see. And this is something that you can only work out yourself?'

'I'm afraid so. Josh, I never meant to lead you on.'

This time he leaned over and kissed her on the shoulder. She shivered with delight. 'You lead me on just by being,' he said. 'Just the sight of you makes my heart beat faster.'

'I wish I could offer you more,' she said.

'So far I'm satisfied. Love grows strongest that grows slow. Now, what are you doing tomorrow? I'm going over to visit my family—my oldest brother's over from New Zealand with his wife and two kids. He's a vet there. And my middle brother is an engineer, he's got three kids. We're having a big family get-together. Fancy coming?'

She looked at him suspiciously. 'Is this some kind of test?'

'Test? Of me or you? I just want you to come along.'

'Well, don't you want to spend some time with your brothers?'

'My brothers are fine. But I need some kind of defence against my mother and sisters-in-law. Give them something to talk about.'

'All right. But make it clear we're just friends.'

'Whatever you say. Now we've got that sorted out, and we're sitting here naked side by side, and we still have plenty of time, why don't we—?'

'No,' she said. Then, a minute later, 'Well, perhaps.'

Cal called her into his room a little later that morning. 'I just wanted to tell you,' he said. 'Something you started yesterday has perhaps the beginnings of a happy ending. Janet Senior, the lady who shouted at you. Not her real name, by the way.'

'I remember her,' Erin said.

'Well, it was you pointing out that perhaps she did have children that worried me. So I phoned the local police inspector who's a mate of mine. He made discreet enquiries at the local caravan sites. I told him the make of the car. He found the lady and her husband and, yes, she did have two children. So he arranged a visit with a social worker—and the kids were promptly taken into care. He's been beating all of them. And the mother is so upset at losing her children that she's decided to lay a charge against him.'

'Is that a happy ending?'

'No. But it might be a happy beginning. You ought to be pleased, Erin.'

She was a bit unsure about meeting Josh's parents and the rest of his family. She badgered him as to what to wear, and he was no use whatsoever. 'I'll be in sports jacket and cords,' he said. 'Wear the female equivalent.'

'What'll you put on your feet?'

'Shoes, of course.' Then he thought and added, 'But I always have a pair of boots in the back of the car anyway.'

So she wore a pretty summer dress and took a bag with jeans, sweater and boots, just in case. When they were driving through Kendal she made him stop and jumped out to buy flowers for his mother and small boxes of chocolates for the children.

'You'll not want to come again,' he told her. 'It'll cost you too much.'

'The money is nothing. It's the worrying that's getting me down.'

Eventually they reached a large farm, pulled up outside the front door and were greeted by eleven people. She knew this, she counted them.

But within minutes she also knew that everything was going to be fine. Josh's mother came and kissed her gently on the cheek and said she was most welcome. 'Please, call me Doreen,' she said. 'Josh, his father and brothers are going to go down the yard and talk about farming things. You come into the kitchen with me,

Amy and Melanie. We're making tea and we can have a little chat.'

'I'll help you make tea,' Erin said.

She might have guessed. There was a great Aga stove in the kitchen and, yes, Josh's mother baked her own bread. Erin set about slicing and buttering it as the other three fetched dishes and set the table. It was a large table in the centre of the kitchen, big enough to seat all of them. Erin liked being with Josh's mother and her two daughters-in-law. She felt that there was a togetherness between them. They were a family.

'We've been asking Josh to come out and visit us in New Zealand,' Amy said to her. 'You know they call it the adventure centre of the world?'

'I've heard, and I'm sure he'd love to come. When he's finished his training.'

'Persuade him to come. And would you come with him? It'd be great to see you both.'

'Amy,' Doreen protested mildly, 'you can't invite Erin to come out with Josh. They're only friends, nothing more.'

'My mistake,' Amy said cheerfully. 'Sorry if I offended you. But if you ever become more than friends, come on out with him.'

'It'd be nice. But I'm not sure that I'm much for adventure now.' Erin bent her head and sawed furiously at the bread she was slicing.

'Don't worry about the adventure. Keep me company while the men do their thing. We've got a guest bungalow, you'd be very welcome.'

Melanie, who lived in England, chimed in, 'We went with the kids and we had a fantastic time. We're looking forward to our next visit.'

'Sounds good,' Erin said. She was thinking that this

was a wonderful family. They were separated by the breadth of the world—but they were obviously still very close to each other.

'I remember you in the school play,' Doreen said after a while. 'Josh made George and I go to see it. We didn't want to at first, we didn't think it would be our sort of thing, but we really enjoyed it. You wore your hair long then—it was lovely.'

'It's still quite long. I...I keep it up because it's handier for work.'

'Let your hair down,' said Amy. 'It's good for a girl.'

It had been decided to feed the children first and put them to bed. It was quite an expedition, going out into the farmyard and persuading them to come in. They were with the men—and wanted to stay there. But their mothers were firm, and in they trooped. Erin joined in the feeding and the bathing and the easing into sleep. She was asked, so she read a story to three of them. But it didn't take long and the five little ones were soon asleep.

'It's the air up here,' Melanie said with satisfaction. 'I always know they're going to sleep.'

Then there was tea for the adults. Erin had been rather worried about this, wondering if anyone would question her presence there, would want to know why Josh had brought her and what their relationship was. She didn't want to answer any questions, she wasn't certain herself. But there had been no need to worry. There were no hints, no indirect queries. She was a guest and she was welcome.

And she was seeing a new Josh. He was at ease with his family, obviously pleased to be with them, at home with them. Earlier on he had been a favourite with the children and they had clung to his hands, asked for his attention. He was a good uncle.

She enjoyed herself and she was sorry when Josh said it was time for them to go. Doreen pressed a parcel into her hands. 'I know you young doctors work very hard,' she said. 'Here's a couple of things I've made that you can eat over the next few days.'

Erin opened her mouth to protest, and then decided not to. 'You will come and see us again?' Doreen went on.

'If I'm invited, I'll come,' Erin promised. And then they were on their way.

CHAPTER SEVEN

IT WAS dusk, it had been a fine day and the evening was beautiful. 'Did you enjoy yourself?' Josh asked.

'You know I did. Josh, you've got a lovely family, I really envy you. It was so…so easy to fit in with them.'

He seemed surprised. 'I suppose so. Aren't all families like that?'

'No,' Erin said. 'I noticed that your mother had three boys, and so far she has five grandchildren—also all boys.'

'These genes,' Josh said, 'they annoy her sometimes. She's very happy with what she's got—but she'd be delighted to have a little girl. We'll get her a daughter some time.'

'I hope so,' Erin said, not liking to consider too deeply the thoughts that his words had provoked. 'Now, Josh, this is a serious question and I want an honest answer. You know I really enjoyed meeting your family. But why did you take me?'

He didn't answer for quite some time. Then he said, 'I think you can tell something about a person by their family. In some ways I am my family—and I'm proud of them. I wanted you to meet them—so you'd know me better.'

'I see,' she said. She was pleased with his reply. But did she want to know him better?

He must have felt this, for his next question was tentative. 'Will you tell me about your family?' he asked.

She hesitated. It was a hard question to answer. 'I'm

an only child, there's just me and my parents. At the moment they're away on a world cruise. They spend much of their life cruising.'

'I thought you had a chemist's shop?'

'My father had three. They were good shops, very well run. But a few years ago he decided to give up work, he sold them for a very high price and retired to a large house in Bournemouth. My mother picked it.'

'Why do I feel that you're giving me some facts but hiding your feelings about them?'

This was difficult. He was right, of course, but perhaps it was disloyal to say what she really felt. But, then, of all people she felt that Josh would understand. And he would be discreet.

'My parents were loving, of course—I suppose they gave me everything I ever needed. But I always felt sort of…extra to them. They both worked tremendously hard on the shops, they were both devoted to their work. Somehow I got a bit left out. I'm not surprised they only had one child, that's all they had time for. When I was ill, they visited me, of course—but when they knew I was recovering they went on the cruise they had booked.'

Erin frowned. 'I'm making something out of nothing. It's just that they never were very demonstrative.'

'You need to show a child that you love her,' he said soberly. 'It's no good hoping that she'll guess.'

'I…I very much liked being with your family just now. They were different to mine, I was welcomed at once. If I ever have a family I want it to be like that.'

'That's quite a compliment.' He thought for a minute. 'When you were at school you were outgoing, confident—nothing bothered you. That's not the behaviour of someone who was uncertain at home.'

'They call it compensation,' she said. 'What I am now is the real me.'

'I think I've still to meet the real you. And I'm looking forward to it because I'm going to love her.'

It wasn't too late when they arrived home. 'We've both got an early start and a full week,' he said, 'but do you fancy a nightcap before you go to bed? I do a mean cocoa.'

'Sounds good. Just for ten minutes, though.' So they went to his living room and in the darkness they both saw the flashing red light. 'Someone's left you a message on your phone,' she said.

They both knew it wouldn't be too urgent. Important calls came through on their mobiles which, as a matter of course, they carried everywhere. Cal insisted on it.

Josh flicked on the recorded message and they both listened. It was from their old school saying that there was to be an open evening in a fortnight's time for those who had left school in the past ten years. There would be a small production by the school dramatic society and a chance to chat afterwards. Was there any chance that Josh could come?

'I'd like to go,' Josh said. 'If I can get away. Will you come, too, Erin? They'll send you an invitation if they know you're here.'

She thought. Did she want to meet classmates from ten years ago, exchange memories and talk about present successes? Did she want to watch younger people on her stage? 'I'm not really sure,' she said.

Josh seemed to understand. 'You don't have to make up your mind at once. Now there's cocoa on the menu.

I know we've been very well fed but could you manage a digestive biscuit as well?'

'Just one, perhaps.'

It was pleasant to sit there beside him on his couch, drinking cocoa and talking about not very much in general. Eventually he put his mug down and slung an arm round her shoulders. She leaned her head against him. It had been a good day. Who knew what the evening would bring?

He kissed her, and it was lovely. She kissed him back and her eyes closed as she sank further into the cushions of the couch. And then her mobile rang.

Both of them looked at it. It was there on the table in front of them. Josh shrugged, then reached over and handed it to her. It was a firm rule in the practice. You always answered your mobile phone.

'Hi, Erin, it's Lyn here,' a cheerful voice said. 'You know you said you'd like to come and help in a home birth? Well, I'm off on one now, and I could do with someone who could help me with the bending and pulling. The lump's getting a bit big. Fancy coming with me? I could pick you up in fifteen minutes.' There was a pause. 'But say no if you've got something on.'

Erin looked at the mournful face Josh was pulling. 'I'll be waiting at the front door,' she said, and rang off. 'Josh, I have to go.'

She walked over to him and took his head in her hands. Then she kissed him quickly on the lips. 'Whatever happens to me, I think I'm blessed in having someone like you,' she said. 'Now I must go and get changed.'

'How many weeks have you been here now?' Josh asked.

It was the next morning. They had met outside their

cottages and were walking smartly together towards the surgery. Erin looked at him cautiously. It wasn't just a casual question. 'Three weeks altogether. Time's running by, I can't understand it.'

'Three weeks. You told me that you came up here to sort your life out, to face up to your problems. How d'you think you're doing?'

'Are you being hard on me, Josh?'

She glanced up at him to see a fleeting look of pain cross his face. 'I could never be hard on you,' he said softly. Then his voice reverted to its previous briskness. 'I only asked. You said there were things you had to do. I wondered how you thought you were progressing.'

'Well, I'm really enjoying the work here. I think I'm gaining confidence dealing with people. Cal, and you, and the rest of the staff, you've been really good for me.'

'Don't you think that David King is at the heart of your problems? Isn't it time you went to see him?'

They walked on in silence. 'I was going to get angry with you,' she said after a while. 'In fact, I still do feel angry. But I know you're only saying it to help me. Why are you so keen to help someone you think has acted badly?'

He remained calm. 'I don't know how you acted. Neither, for that matter, do you. All we have is David's account of things, and I've met better witnesses in my time. The question is, are you happy with things as they are?'

'No. I'd rather have all my teeth out without gas than go to see David, but I know I've got to. As soon as we get to the surgery I'll phone him.' Suddenly her morning didn't seem as fine as it had done before.

'I'd very much like to come with you,' Josh said.

She had never imagined this. 'Why? Do you think I can't fight for myself? D'you think I'll get talked into something I don't want? I'm a big girl now, you know.'

'Everyone needs help sometimes,' he said.

'I'm not sure I want you there when we're arguing. Because I know we're going to argue.'

'Having a third party there will calm things down. And you need someone dispassionate to be on your side, someone as an observer.'

'So you're going to be my dispassionate observer?'

'I'd much rather be your passionate lover,' he murmured, and she blushed.

They had reached the surgery gates. 'There's five minutes before the morning get-together,' she said. 'I'll phone David now. Probably I'll get through to his mother.'

It was Mrs King who answered and she was not friendly. 'We had been expecting a call from you long before this. David's been so concerned. And after that other doctor called...'

'I've been very busy. I've just started this new job,' Erin said. She felt angry with herself for feeling that she had to offer excuses, but the words had somehow slipped out. 'I thought I might call round on Wednesday afternoon.'

'I'll just have to see if I'm in.' There was a long pause. Erin knew that David's mother was so well organised that she could account for every minute over the next ten weeks. But Erin must be made to suffer a little. 'Yes, Wednesday will be fine. Do I take it that you'll be making some kind of decisions about the future?'

'This is purely a social call,' Erin said. 'One old acquaintance meeting another.' Then she rang off.

She met Josh again as they entered the doctors' coffee-lounge. 'You're a bit white-faced,' he said. 'I'm sorry if your phone call wasn't a happy one.'

'I never thought it would be.'

For the next two and a half days Erin found herself dreading the meeting. On the Tuesday night she hardly slept at all and for the first time in weeks she had the nightmare. What was going to be decided? And what made it worse was that Josh was going to be there. What would he think about her when it was demonstrated that she was the kind of woman who would abandon a fiancé when he needed her? She wasn't looking forward to that at all.

But when she looked back at her previous relationship with David, it had never been very deep. They had gone for long periods without seeing each other. She knew he'd had a long string of girlfriends at university. When they'd met in the holidays it had often been because there had been no other friends to go out with. Why had she accepted his proposal?

'I think we should go in my car,' Josh said when they met on Wednesday afternoon. 'I don't want you getting into a rage and driving us both off the road.'

'You seem to think this is some kind of joke!'

'I don't at all. I'm just trying to keep some sense of proportion. Too much anger, too much emotion—they stop people thinking clearly.'

It was clear what Mrs King thought when they presented themselves at the front door. 'We didn't expect to see you here, Dr Harrison, not after last time. Do you want to go for a drive round for a couple of hours? Or do I have to find a room where you can sit?'

'Dr Harrison's coming in to see David with me,' Erin said.

'Is he? I don't think that's a very good idea at all.'

'If he doesn't go in, neither do I.'

Erin was determined not to be dominated by this bitter older woman. For a while they stared at each other in silence. Mrs King dropped her eyes first.

'I don't like it but I'll see what David says. Wait here.'

She was left in the hall with Josh. His face remained impassive but he nodded at her encouragingly. So far she was not doing too badly.

The door at the end of the hall was wrenched open. 'In here,' Mrs King snapped. 'And, please, be as…polite as you can. He's suffered, you know.'

Erin remembered the room. The Kings had always believed in entertaining as many of the local gentry as they could attract, David had brought her to the odd cocktail party here. And there he was, lying on a couch with a rug over his legs. An electric wheelchair stood by the couch.

His voice was as cordial as it had ever been. 'Erin, good to see you! Sorry I can't get up but…' He held out his hand.

She went over to shake his hand. The moment he had hold of her he pulled her forward to try to kiss her. Unbalanced, she fell forward and had to press against his chest to straighten herself. He wouldn't let go. She didn't want to kiss him and there was a short and un-dignified struggle before she managed to straighten herself.

'No kiss for an old friend?' he asked reproachfully.

She decided to ignore the question. She didn't want an argument—well, not yet. 'How are you, David?'

He waved towards his legs, hidden by the blanket. 'I

have been considerably better.' He went on, 'I thought that when you phoned you'd be coming on your own. Why is Dr Harrison with you?'

'He's a friend.'

'I see.' David looked blackly at Josh. 'I suppose it would be too much to ask you to leave us alone for a while? This is a private conversation.'

'I will happily leave,' Josh said, and Erin saw David's face light up. But after a pause Josh went on, 'If Erin asks me to.'

'Erin?' David questioned.

'Dr Harrison is another doctor and a friend of mine. I want him to stay. He may be able to help.'

'I'm a person, not a case! I don't need a doctor, I don't need help. Anyway, what's your relationship with this man? When I asked him he wouldn't tell me, said I had to ask you.'

'My relationships are none of your business. I didn't come here to talk about them, I came here to help.'

'And how d'you propose to do that?'

Holding onto her courage, Erin said, 'The accident was some time ago. I would have thought that by now you would be used to your prosthesis. I expected to see you walking.'

'Well, I'm not! It's not as easy as you people with two legs think!'

Erin felt she was drowning in a sea of accusations and bitterness. No matter what she said, David managed to twist it. It was impossible to talk to him. She was grateful when Josh broke in.

'We have a bit of a problem,' Josh said. 'As you know, after the accident Erin lost her memory. Only you know what happened, only you know that you got engaged.'

David smiled. He had power again. 'Yes, I know what happened. I remember very clearly.'

'Do you expect Erin to agree to something she has no memory of?'

'Losing her memory was very convenient. Sometimes I wonder if she'd have lost it if I had two legs.'

Then David looked up and saw that he had angered both of them. Quickly he backed down. 'But I guess she's not faking.'

He looked at Erin, his face now calm and reasonable again. 'I've told you this before, I don't mind going over it again. Lord knows, I go over and over it again myself.'

He settled himself under his blanket. 'We were walking together near Red Tarn. It was a gorgeous day, we were both intensely happy. We'd been thinking about this for quite some time, now I was working and you were nearly qualified it seemed a good idea. Everybody expected it. I'd bought a ring. I asked you to marry me, you agreed at once. The ring was too loose, so I said I'd have it altered to fit. Erin, we were engaged.'

It was hard not to believe him, he was so earnest, so persuasive. She felt herself wondering. Could she have agreed? For a while had she thought that her future happiness could be with this man?

'I just can't see it happening,' she said half to herself. 'We never had that kind of relationship.'

'You're trying to avoid your responsibilities. It was you who dragged me up Striding Edge, you said we had to do something else mad. Then we both fell but I was the one who broke a leg. I must be the only man ever to be engaged for less than an hour.'

'What do you want me to do?' she asked, her voice quavering.

'Act honourably. We're engaged. Nothing will ever

persuade me otherwise. In time, when I've recovered, we'll get married. But I'll never recover until I know I have you.'

He took a box from the table in front of her, threw it at her. 'Here's the ring. Take it, and when you look at it think of what you've done.'

The ring hit her arm, fell to the floor. 'Pick it up, pick it up!' David screamed.

Josh stepped forward and picked it up. 'I'll see that she gets it,' he said. 'But for now I think we should be going.'

'I don't want to see you again! And she can come back when she's willing to face up to her responsibilities.'

A silent but obviously seething Mrs King showed them out. They climbed into Josh's car. 'I'm sorry you had to go through that scene,' Erin said after ten minutes.

'Well, now we all know where we stand,' Josh said. 'You're in a turmoil I know,' he said. 'Your emotions are churned up and you feel like shouting at someone— I'll do because I'm nearest. I suggest that we say nothing now. We've both got evening surgery soon—that'll take our minds off things. And afterwards, this evening, instead of going to my place or yours, why don't we go for a walk? We can talk at the same time.'

'Why do you always have to be so calm and reasonable? Perfect people make me sick!'

'I'm not perfect,' he said.

Then there was silence for a while, until her conscience got the better of her and she said, 'Sorry. That was uncalled for. And you've been such a help to me.'

'That's OK.' He patted her leg in a friendly fashion. 'I guess you're not perfect either. But you're close.'

'You'll never know how wrong you are,' she told him.

Surprisingly, Erin enjoyed her evening surgery. She was able to forget her own troubles and concentrate on those of the people who came to sit at the side of her desk. There was the usual collection of minor ailments, recurrent problems, possible serious complaints. She wrote out repeat prescriptions, told a pregnant mother that there was little to be done about the nausea but to go to see the midwife. She prescribed an ointment for the bloodshot eye of a young child and reassured the mother that, no, her baby wasn't going blind. She referred two people to hospital, but told them that there might be quite a wait. She counselled a woman who had started on HRT, and was having unfortunate side effects. All part of a GP's job, and so much that she enjoyed.

Afterwards she went home, changed into jeans and a loose jacket and put on a pair of stout shoes. Then she waited for Josh to call for her.

He was on time. 'A twenty-minute ride,' he said. 'And then I've picked a riverside walk. It should be quiet at this time of year, and there are no cliffs, no sudden drops to scare you.'

'Just what I need. Peace and gentle exercise.'

'And the chance to talk. That's the purpose of the entire exercise.'

'Sometimes I think I'm tired of talking and getting nowhere. But I suppose you're right. Take me to this quiet walk.'

It was only a twenty-minute ride and then they strolled side by side down a river path, listening to the gurgling of the water and the odd bird cry. The heat of summer was now over, but the sun still shone through the leaves, dappling the path in front of them.

For a while she was happy to walk in silence. He took

her hand and walked in silence, too, obviously happy to let her set the pace.

'What are we talking about this time?' she asked abruptly. 'What do we have to decide and how does it affect you?'

He didn't reply at once and she could tell by the anxious way he glanced around him that he was trying to be absolutely precise. Eventually he said, 'We're talking about us. I think we're talking about something that grew between the two of us without either of us wanting it. When we met for the first time in ten years, we were both wary. For different reasons neither of us wanted a relationship. And yet we were drawn to each other.'

'We went to bed,' she said.

'I know we did. It was the most magic moment of my life and I suspect I'll think of it the day I'm dying. But making love to you meant we jumped into something we weren't ready for. After Annabelle I was cautious. Perhaps all I wanted was a physical relationship—something that brought both a little comfort but with no great commitment on either side. Something quickly over.'

'You didn't think you were having that with me?' She was curious.

'Never,' he said laconically. 'I knew you were a woman who wanted total commitment or nothing. And that's what I want with you.'

'So what do you want of me now? I suppose I'm being a bit arrogant, demanding that you talk first. It must make you feel…feel vulnerable.'

Josh laughed. 'You've made me feel far more vulnerable than Annabelle ever did, but for some odd reason I don't mind. Give me a minute to think a bit more.'

They strode on for another hundred yards and then he said, 'I'll tell you what I want of you now. First I want you to be free of guilt. All this rubbish about David—it doesn't matter whether you said you'd marry him or not. I doubt you ever did. David isn't holding you back, Erin—you're holding yourself back. When you're free of that guilt I want to see an awful lot more of you. And I think you're the woman I've been looking for all my life.'

'I'm not the girl you remember from school, Josh. I was till the accident. But I suffered subdural haemorrhage, both the neurologist and the psychiatrist said that there could be some quite major character changes.'

He stopped, took her in his arms and kissed her gently. 'The golden girl I remember is still there. I know it. And soon she'll be back. I'll know it. And I love her.'

'I hope she'll be back,' Erin said.

She went to bed early and lay there, thinking about the day. First, the interview with David. It had shredded her nerves, it had been a repetition of other visits that she had endured before. She had come back to Keldale hoping to free herself of the guilt, hoping that David would see that there was no future in persecuting her. If she could only remember! But just the knowledge that he was lying there, refusing to help himself, filled her with self-doubt. Had she brought him to this?

Next, the walk with Josh. How did she feel about Josh? She wriggled in bed, feeling the sheets rub against her bare thighs and arms, remembering how it had felt when he had held her. He had carried her off to a place she'd never known existed, a paradise of physical delight that was the more wonderful because it was with a man whom she…loved?

'Do I love Josh?' Daringly, she spoke the words aloud to herself. It was the first time she had ever thought about it in such alarmingly honest terms. And when she did so the answer seemed simple. Yes, she did.

What did Josh feel for her? She thought now about the walk by the river, how he had striven to be honest with her. He had said he loved her—or the girl she used to be. She guessed that would be a word he would not use lightly. To say he loved her would mean a serious commitment to him.

But he had said that she was the woman he had been looking for all his life. That was something.

He wanted her to be free of guilt; more than that, to be the woman—or girl—that he remembered. Could she ever change? Could she become confident again, free of guilt about David, able to look at the high crags of Lakeland and see their beauty instead of being racked by fear? She hoped so.

But then there was her small flat in London, the job in medicine. Would these make her happier? Certainly they wouldn't test her as much.

Erin sighed. It was all so difficult.

Just before she drifted off to sleep a stray thought struck her, something that had nothing to do with her previous thoughts. Cassie Beynon, the social worker she and Josh had argued with about the future of Barry Keith. Her character showed in her behaviour—she was full of energy, she had to keep moving. Why did she limp so badly? Erin slept.

Next morning, when she had ten minutes to herself, Erin shut herself in her room and phoned Cassie Beynon. The reason she gave was that it was a general follow-up call about Barry Keith.

'It took some doing but he's all right now,' Cassie said. 'I managed to find him a vacancy at a place called

Kale View Rest Home. He's happy there. Seeing a few more people has made him come out a bit more. I have to admit, you were right and I was wrong. He needed supervised attention at once.'

'I'm glad he's doing well,' Erin said. 'And we do appreciate the trouble you went to to find him a place.'

'It's my job,' Cassie said with a laugh. 'How's that gorgeous partner of yours?'

'Josh? He's doing well. He'll be glad to hear Barry is OK.'

'Good. Have you two got over your lovers' tiff yet?'

'What?'

Cassie laughed again. 'There was a definite coolness between the two of you when we met. And you only get that kind of coolness when the two people concerned have been very close.'

Erin realised that Cassie was much more shrewd than she had at first appeared.

'Cassie, I'm going to ask you something personal. You have every right to tell me to mind my own business. When we met, I saw that you limped. D'you mind telling me why?'

Cassie's answer was prompt. 'Course I don't mind telling you. It's something I usually tell people straight away so they're not embarrassed and neither am I. I've got an artificial leg. A silly motorbike accident when I was younger than I am now and had less sense. Any special reason you want to know?'

'I need your help,' Erin said.

CHAPTER EIGHT

IT WAS odd, going back to her old school. Everything was so much the same—and so different. Erin wandered through the corridors side by side with Josh and they looked, paused and remembered.

'This is the biology lab,' she said, peering through the doorway. 'I remember in the third year that Miss Hollis dissected a real rabbit for us. We thought it was terrible! The neat little coloured diagrams in our books were much nicer.'

'I remember those diagrams. I had the same problem in medical school. When I dissected my cadaver, the body looked nothing like the way the book said it should. I complained to the supervisor and he said that the body had served its owner well for seventy years so it must be some good.'

Erin giggled. 'It's the difference between art and life,' she said.

There were others moving around, looking in classrooms, whispering memories to each other. And some of the older schoolchildren were there to act as guides.

'Are you allowed to wear black trousers as part of your uniform?' Erin asked one of the girls in amazement. She remembered the old assistant head, who had had special responsibility for female welfare. 'Mrs Leggat must be horrified.'

'Mrs Leggat suggested it.' The girl smiled. 'Said we had to move with the times.'

'Remarkable. I wouldn't have believed it. Does she still wear the same length skirts?'

'Never above mid-calf. But she has been seen teaching in a pair of smart tan trousers.'

Erin shivered. Was everything changing?

'Erin, come and look here.' There was something slightly odd about Josh's voice. He had strolled a few yards ahead and was looking at some kind of display on the wall. She walked up to him and he pointed.

The display was of plays the school had put on over the past years. And Josh was pointing to a set of pictures of *Romeo and Juliet*. There Erin was, hair cascading down over her shoulders, dressed in a blue velvet gown with white lace at the neck. She was looking up adoringly at Romeo, in doublet and hose. David King.

The schoolgirl to whom she'd been talking had followed her. Now she looked at the picture, then glanced at Erin. 'That's you!' she said. 'You haven't changed much, have you? Is your hair still as long?'

'I wear it tied back because I'm a doctor. It gets in my way.'

'You look lovely in the picture.'

Erin studied the photograph, tried to remember how she had felt ten years ago, what she had felt for David King. She knew that Josh was watching her. 'Happy memories?' he asked gently.

'Life was simpler then.' She looked at the picture again. 'I don't remember feeling anything really special for David, though. We were just part of the same group.'

'Erin, I've been looking for you everywhere. I'm so glad you've come. Look, I've a favour to ask you.'

Erin blinked and turned. There behind her was Miss Cole and Eunice. Erin had been to a couple of the meetings of the local amateur dramatic society and had enjoyed working with Miss Cole again, but felt that she just could not guarantee the time to take part in any production.

'Anything I can do to help, Miss Cole,' she said. 'How's the hip?'

Miss Cole impatiently waved her Zimmer frame to show that her hip was all right. 'It's fine, fine. Now, in twenty minutes we're going to see the drama display. Four short plays, they'll only take about an hour. It's to be a competition. There were to be three judges but one has phoned to say that she can't make it and so I'm co-opting you. There's the manager of the local rep and myself, and we thought that the star of one of the most successful productions of recent years would be a fine third judge. That's you. Come along, we'll be starting soon.'

Erin turned in bewilderment to Josh. 'I can't think of anyone better suited,' he said loudly. 'Miss Cole, may I judge the scene shifters?'

Miss Cole fixed him with a steely eye. 'Thanks for volunteering,' she said. 'I'll mark you down as a judge at the next drama festival.'

Erin found herself being swept away.

It was strange to find herself again in the great hall of the school, to see the stage with its curtains drawn. She remembered the view from the back of the curtain, the dry-mouthed feeling that soon all eyes on the other side of the curtain would be fixed on her.

She was introduced to the new drama mistress and the new head. The headmistress promptly asked her to come and talk to the school about career opportunities in medicine for girls.

'I'll bring my colleague,' Erin said. 'He can do the same for the boys.'

With the other three judges she was given a seat with a desk and a light. 'We don't just announce a winner,' Miss Cole told her. 'This is an adjudication as well as a competition. We comment on everything.' She went on, 'I'm not going on stage with my Zimmer and poor Mr Bowling, the rep manager, has got a cold. So you'll have to deliver our results.'

'Stand on that stage and talk to all those people!'

'The last time you stood on that stage you were a fantastic success.'

'But, Miss Cole, that was some time ago and now I'm—'

'A skill like yours is never lost. Now, sit and watch.'

The plays started. Erin sat and watched and scribbled notes and tried to forget what was to come. And she became interested. All four plays were well done, but one she felt was a clear winner. The trouble was, the undoubted best actor was in one of the other plays. But there was something good to say about everything.

Fortunately, Miss Cole and Mr Bowling agreed with her conclusions. They spent five minutes deciding what she would say, and then she was sent to stand on stage and face the audience.

It had all happened too quickly. She was fine talking to a patient in the surgery, fine addressing a small group of pregnant mums. But now she was isolated, alone, she just didn't have the confidence. There was a momentary flash of real fear—for a second she was tumbling down that mountainside again, entirely out of control.

She stood at the lectern provided in the centre of the stage, looked from her notes to the sea of anonymous faces in front of her. She couldn't do this! She would have to run into the wings and then face the ridicule of everyone.

When she had walked to the lectern the audience had quickly quietened. Now she heard a rising hum of conversation—people were wondering why she didn't start. And that made things worse.

What should she do? The words just wouldn't come. She was trapped here on stage and the longer she stayed silent the harder it would be to begin.

Then, from somewhere, she remembered what Miss Cole had said to her, perhaps fifteen years ago, when she had first started with the drama club. 'Don't worry about the audience. Fix on one person in the fifth row and speak to him. The rest will hear perfectly well.'

Fix on a person in the fifth row. Desperately she scanned the rows in front of her. Not him, not her, not her, not him…yes, him. She saw Josh smiling at her encouragingly, and she knew that he knew what she was feeling. But she could speak to Josh all right. He was her friend.

'Ladies and gentlemen,' she started confidently, 'it's ten years since I last stood on this stage, and I feel…' Her words echoed through the hall. Things would go well now.

It was still an exhausting evening. When Josh was driving her home later she leaned back in her seat and sighed. 'One reunion every ten years,' she said. 'That will be quite enough.'

He stretched an arm out to caress her shoulders. 'You were brilliant,' he said. 'When you talked you caught the audience just as you used to. But you should have let your hair down.'

'There are two meanings to that. When I climbed on that stage I was terrified, Josh. I thought I wasn't going to be able to do it. Then I saw you, and you gave me confidence.'

'The confidence came from yourself,' he said softly.

Erin hadn't really expected to hear anything from Cassie Beynon, so she was surprised when she received a phone call at the surgery a week later just before her lunch-break.

'David King,' Cassie said after the usual exchange of greetings. 'I know I thought that you and Josh were close, but is David your fiancé or not? I need to know.'

'He's not my fiancé. He never has been. We've never been more than good friends. And we're not really that now.'

'That's what I thought. Only I've been getting mixed messages from him about you.'

David is good at mixing messages, Erin thought, but she didn't say so. 'Has he been talking about me?' she asked.

'I get the impression that you're not his favourite person. He thinks you've treated him badly but now he's willing to forgive you. If you meet again in the future he'll be polite but that will be all. He's putting you and your relationship behind him.'

'He's doing what?'

Cassie sounded sheepish. 'That's why I needed to know if you thought you were still engaged to him. I don't go round stealing other people's fiancés. We've been out to dinner a couple of times. The first time I more or less dragged him out, the second time he asked me. And…things are progressing.'

'Cassie, I asked you to go round because I thought David needed help. You've come to terms with having an artificial leg, he hadn't. I thought perhaps that if he talked to you, if he saw that an attractive young person could have a good active life, then…' Erin realised she was missing the main point. 'David is not, not, not my fiancé.'

'Good.'

Erin was having difficulty understanding this, it was the last thing she had expected. 'Are you seriously interested in him?' she asked. 'I wouldn't want you to think that I... That is, do you know what he's really like?'

Cassie laughed again. 'You mean that he's vain, self-dramatising and self-pitying? Of course I know what he's like. He's also very insecure. I can help him with that. I think that underneath he's quite a nice man and that when I've worked on him for a while he'll be a lot happier.'

'I wish you all the luck in the world,' Erin said. 'And you're right, there is a nice man somewhere underneath.' She thought for a moment. 'Have you met his mother yet?'

'Now, there's a challenge,' Cassie said.

Erin knew Josh was in the building so she went in search of him to tell him this news.

'So that is the last thing I expected to happen,' she said as she finished recounting her conversation with Cassie. 'But I'm so glad. Cassie will be good for David, David will be happy and I...I'm...'

'Because of your own efforts you're free of something that was dragging you down,' he said. 'Don't you feel an awful lot better?'

'I certainly do. But I didn't plan it this way.'

'But you worked towards it.' His voice was abstracted, as if he was puzzling over something else. 'And if there hadn't been that push...'

He appeared to make up his mind about something.

'Erin, it's lunchtime. Can we walk outside for half an hour? There's something I need to tell you and I'd like to do it…well, away from people.'

'Away from people? A confession? Do you expect me to start yelling and screaming?'

'You might feel you're entitled to. But I thought it was in your best interests.'

'Sounds ominous. But at the moment I'm in such a good temper that I think I'd forgive you anything.'

It was a mild early autumnal day, the leaves were just starting to change colour and they walked behind the surgery along a quiet lane that led into the hills.

'You were feeling guilty about David,' he said. 'I thought there was no need for it and I wanted you to accept there was no need, and not worry whether you'd agreed to marry him or not.'

'I suspect it doesn't matter now.'

'I agree.' He took a breath. 'Now I'm going to tell you that I know you didn't agree to marry him. When he found out that you'd lost your memory he decided to make up a story—to lie, if you like.'

She looked at him in astonishment. 'How can you say that? You can't possibly know.'

'In fact, I can.' From his pocket Josh took a small box. With a shock Erin recognised it as the box containing the engagement ring. She remembered David had thrown it on the floor and Josh had picked it up.

'I've carried this with me since David threw it. I started to think and I made a few enquiries. Every day I've wondered, should I tell you or not? It hasn't been easy, Erin.'

'Never mind that. How d'you know David was lying?'

'You told me the date of your accident—the date David proposed, put this ring on your finger.'

He opened the case, pointed to the name and address of the Kendal jeweller, printed in the lid of the box. 'I was suspicious from the start. I took the ring back to the shop where it was bought. The jeweller looked up his records and found that it had been purchased five weeks after your accident.'

She stood bewildered. 'He bought the ring after he knew I'd lost my memory! He didn't propose to me, he made it all up afterwards! So it was all part of a nasty plan. Josh, that is so low!'

He shrugged. 'Emotionally damaged people can do unpleasant things. It isn't fair to blame them. I've no doubt that when David threw this ring at you, he had convinced himself that he was the injured party and you had wronged him.'

'Possibly,' she said pensively. They walked on in silence for a while and then she said, 'You knew this, you knew how it would comfort me and yet you didn't tell me. That was cruel! I had a right to know!'

Josh's face looked haggard. 'I know. But I wanted you to... I thought it better if you... You had to come to terms with the guilt yourself. Free yourself of it. The facts weren't important.'

'They were important to me and I had a right to know,' she said. 'Do you know the suffering you've put me through?'

'I suffered myself.'

'Possibly.' They walked on a while then she said, 'I think I'd like you to stay here and I'll walk back to the surgery by myself. I've had a shock and I want to think about myself—and about you.'

'As you wish.'

He stood still as she turned. Even in her anger she could still appreciate how he would leave her space to think, no matter what he might want to say in his own defence.

Erin's first reaction had been horror at what David had done, her second reaction anger at Josh for keeping it from her. But as she headed back to the surgery, she recognised that Josh had only done what he had thought best for her. And perhaps he was right. She should be strong enough to think of herself, not be blackmailed by what might have happened.

But the fact remained that Josh had known she was suffering pain and had had the means to spare her, thinking it was better for her he leave her to work out her own salvation. Was she strong enough to live with a man who had such iron ideas about how to live?

Her afternoon surgery was largely uneventful. But her last patient was Mrs Brice, and Mrs Brice was a case. She was forty-five, overweight, a single mother of four children and had a stressful job at which she was very good. All this she told Erin, and much more besides. She had told her the same story on the last two visits, a week and a fortnight before.

Erin listened to her heart, slipped on the sphygmomanometer, took the reading and winced. Blood pressure was way too high. Mrs Brice was hypertensive.

'Do you take your pills regularly, Mrs Brice?'

'Yes, Doctor. Well, I might miss the occasional one. After all, they don't seem to do much for me, do they?'

'Not taking them could have very unfortunate effects. Now, how about your diet? Making sure you have the five pieces of fruit a day? Managing to cut down on smoking?'

'Oh, yes.' Mrs Brice smiled, obviously and amiably lying.

'And exercise?'

'I'm walking quite a bit more.'

'Mrs Brice, I don't think you realise just how serious this condition can be.'

It was always difficult, persuading someone who only had the most minor symptoms that they had to radically alter their lifestyle. But with as much conviction as she could, Erin talked about diet, exercise, stress management, cutting down on smoking and alcohol. And as she went through the possible consequences of not taking care, Erin saw that she was getting through. If not afraid, Mrs Brice was at least aware. 'You have to think of what your children would do if you were ill,' Erin concluded.

I'm getting there, Erin thought as she showed a frowning Mrs Brice out of her room. I can be assertive about some things.

When she got home that night she phoned Josh. He was only next door but she wanted the distance that the phone would give. She needed to talk to him and not to have to see him.

'I think I upset you,' she said. 'But now I realise you were only thinking of me, I'm sorry I got angry.'

'Erin, you should know that I wouldn't deliberately hurt you for anything.'

'I know that. But your determination always to do what is right—I respect you for it but sometimes it's hard to live with.'

'I know I've got faults,' he said. There was such desolation in his voice that she felt instantly sorry.

'D'you want to come round?' she asked. 'Just for five minutes. I didn't want to see you, I wanted to keep my distance.'

'All right. Is this something special we're to talk about?'

'Just come round.'

So they sat opposite each other in her living room. Josh was not his usual calm self. Erin thought he looked worried. She felt worried herself.

'I think our relationship—whatever it is—is coming to some kind of crisis,' she said. 'We both need to make some kind of commitment—or have none at all.'

'I agree,' he said. She could tell he wasn't going to help her.

'It's a responsibility for me. I know what you suffered over Annabelle. I'm not going to see you hurt again. And I'm afraid of hurting you without intending to.'

'It's a risk.' He frowned, took out his diary. 'Look, we need to get things sorted. We've both got Sunday free, let's spend it together. If the weather is good we'll go on a low-level walk, if it's really good we'll go out on the lake. We'll talk and we'll settle things. OK?'

'That suits me fine.'

He came over, kissed her gently on the cheek. 'I hope things go well,' he whispered.

Only when he had gone did she shiver. She wondered if he knew what he was asking her, inviting her to walk. He didn't feel it, couldn't ever understand it. To look at heights, even from a distance, still terrified her.

When Josh called for Erin on Sunday morning he was dressed casually in T-shirt and light trousers—not his heavier walking clothes. 'Where's your climbing kit?' she asked.

'In the boot, of course. It's quite a warm day, I thought we'd just be tourists.'

She liked him for that, he was thinking of her. 'That's great. Give me a minute, I'll go and change. I'll bring my heavier stuff with me.'

So she went and put on her shorts, and felt much better.

It was an odd day. The sun was out but there appeared to be a haze in the sky. There was no wind and the air felt lethargic. It was not a good day for walking.

She felt melancholy, almost resigned. Hopeful, of course—but she suspected that when the day was over, her life would have changed. For better or worse, she didn't know. But today she was determined to make a decision.

They had only been driving for twenty minutes when his mobile rang. He frowned. 'I'm not on call,' he muttered, and pulled into a handy layby.

'Oh, hi, Ben... Left what? I'll have a quick look.'

He turned in his seat and scrabbled in the rear footwell. When he sat upright again Erin saw that he was holding a pair of light rock-climbing boots, expensive ones with bright purple laces. She knew that only the experts wore them.

'Yes, they're here. No, I'll bring them to you... Not much of a diversion if you're on Flinder's Edge... It's no trouble.'

He put down the phone, started the car and pulled out. 'Ben Halley, a friend of mine,' he explained. 'I gave him a lift home last week and he left his boots in the car. I said I'd drop them off to him—it'll only be fifteen minutes or so. You don't mind, do you?'

In fact, she did mind. The last thing she wanted was to be faced with anything that needed climbing. But she said, no, there was no problem.

Shortly afterwards they drove off the main road onto a minor road and then up a rough track. Ahead of her, bleak and dark, she could see a cliff edge. She tried not to look at it, but it was everywhere. Perhaps her fear showed on her face, but Josh was too busy negotiating the track to notice.

'Not many people have climbed on the Edge,' he told her as they neared it. 'We're putting up a lot of new routes, trying to write a guide. You'll see it in a minute.'

They got to the Edge, it was in shadow. She could tell that it would see very little sun. It looked greasy, running with moisture. And it was almost vertical. Her breath stuck in her throat as she saw the height of it. Two men, in the brightly coloured outfits the climbers often now wore, were perched precariously on the rock.

Josh pointed to a dark fissure that ran from the bottom to the top of the Edge. 'See that crack? I led it for the first time last week. That means I can name it. I'd like to name it after you. Do you mind?'

Erin saw the crack and the thought of Josh climbing it horrified her. But she managed to mumble something about being delighted if it was named after her.

Expertly skipping from rock to rock, another climber ran towards them. 'Good of you to come, Josh. Thanks for the boots.'

'Not at all. Ben, a friend of mine, Erin Hunter.'

Ben beamed and shook hands. 'Pleased to meet you, Erin. Are you a climber, too?'

She said that she wasn't, that she walked a little.

'That's a pity. Josh here is an expert. No time for a quick one, Josh?'

She saw him look at the Edge, saw the intent expression on his face. But he said no.

She said, 'Go for a climb if you want, Josh. I'll sit here in the car and read my book.'

'No. We've got plenty to do ourselves.' He said good-bye to Ben and they bumped back down the track.

'I wouldn't have minded if you'd gone for a climb,' she said after five minutes.

'Yes, you would have minded,' he said gently. 'I know it. I saw your face.'

It took them twenty minutes to get to Glenridding, at the head of Ullswater. Erin noticed that it was rather busy as it was towards the end of the tourist season and people were obviously hoping for a last good day before autumn truly set in.

'I thought we might hire a rowing boat for the day,' he said. 'I had a row on Derwentwater a few weeks ago and I enjoyed it.'

'Sounds a good idea.'

So they carried the picnic basket to the marina and hired a boat. She made him slap on the sunblock as the hazy sun was unusually powerful. There was still no wind and the few sailing boats out were becalmed.

He set off to row to the opposite bank and soon they were in the middle of the lake. He was strong, fit and not rowing too hard, but within minutes the sweat was beaded on his face. She was warm herself. She took a handkerchief from her pocket, dipped it in the lake and offered it to him to cool his face. He accepted gratefully, and for a minute leaned on his oars.

'Look at the view,' he said, 'you can see Hart Crag and High Dodd.' He pulled on one oar, spun the boat round. 'And there is…Helvellyn. You can even see the top of Striding Edge.'

Then he looked at her speculatively. 'Of course, that's where you had your accident.'

'On Striding Edge,' she agreed.

She looked at his contented face. He was happy out here. He belonged. She knew he could not be happy unless surrounded by his mountains, and there was noth-

ing she could do about it. Without a conscious thought
she discovered that her mind was made up. Too much
held them apart. A calmness, a sense of resignation fell
on her. They must part. She could always go back to
London. But she would have today.

'I'm getting hungry,' she said, and he pulled for the
far shore.

They found a tiny beach. Josh spread a blanket on it
and then unloaded the picnic basket he had packed himself. She saw the trouble he had gone to, and felt more
sad than ever at the news she was going to have to give
him.

They ate for a while. Then he said, 'Well, are we
going to talk?'

'Not yet. I'm happy now. I want this to carry on for
a little longer.'

But she knew by the look he gave her that he had
guessed what she was going to say, and that he was sad,
too.

She reached for his hand. Holding hands meant nothing. But as she did so he moved away and rose to look
over the lake. A cool breeze swept across her and suddenly she felt cold. She realised he hadn't stood to avoid
her, he was intent on something else.

'Let's get in the boat,' he said. 'I want to row back.
I don't like the look of the weather, I think there's a
squall coming. We don't want to be stuck on this side
of the lake.'

Quickly they gathered things together and threw them
into the boat. Then he was rowing strongly back to the
marina. It was strange how quickly things changed. The
wind was chill, there were ripples on the water.
Occasionally rain spotted down and the surrounding hills
were now blanketed in cloud. She couldn't see the sum-

mit of Helvellyn. As he rowed, she packed the picnic box.

The boatman at the marina was pleased they had returned but was worried about the other boats. 'Hope they have the sense to come back as well,' he said. 'But some people have no sense.'

The rain was getting harder now and they scurried to where Josh had parked the car. It was cold, too. They fetched their bags out of the boot and quickly changed in the car. It felt good to be warm. And just as they finished changing there was a rattle on the roof and the rain sluiced down.

Josh drove out of Glenridding and after five minutes took a small road to where they could park. 'Silly to drive in this,' he said. They sat side by side and watched the rain sweeping across the fields, felt the wind buffeting the car. They were in a little world of greyness. And for a while they were silent.

Josh broke the silence. His voice was gentle. 'You have something to tell me, haven't you? Erin, I'll accept whatever you wish. You decide about us.'

'You're not going to try to persuade me?'

'Erin, I've never been a bully, either physically or emotionally, I'm not going to start now. I think you've been bullied enough over the past two years. Only one thing. We must decide now. Either we are a couple, like other couples, trying to sort out our differences, see where we are going. Or we are friends and colleagues. As we were, as we intended to be. But if you tell me that there's to be nothing more then never again will we…be as close as we have been.'

At first she couldn't trust herself to speak. Then she said, 'I can't see us having a happy future. I think you're a marvellous man, the best I've ever met. But we're so different, I couldn't make you happy.'

She waved at the grey scene outside. 'This world is your life. You're even happy now in the rain. But I hate it, it terrifies me. And we're two different kinds of people. You're confident, you know what you want. And I don't. Josh, we have to part. We could never live together.'

He didn't reply. She looked at him as he stared out of the window, wondered if he realised that she was doing this as much for him as for herself. He turned to her and was about to speak when his phone rang.

How often had her life been interfered with by a mobile phone?

He looked angrily at the little screen. 'It's the surgery,' he said. 'I'm not on call, I'm not going to answer.'

'Of course you are. It might be important.'

So he did. 'Oh, hi, Cal… Near Glenridding… Lucky for who?' Then Erin heard his voice deepen, become serious. 'How many? We need professionals… I see. Striding Edge! OK, I've got all my gear, give me the grid reference.' He groped for a pen and paper. 'I know it, but I've got my satellite navigator with me, too.'

Without speaking he put down the phone and started the car, and they lurched forward, taking the road back to Glenridding.

'Did I hear you say Striding Edge?' she asked after a while. 'What's happening on Striding Edge?' Erin knew her voice was high, she couldn't help it.

'A party of schoolchildren, aged about fourteen. They were on their way down, the weather broke and they came off route. There was a bit of a slide. They're all a bit battered but the worst injured is the man in charge. He seems quite competent but he's broken his leg and has head injuries. Second in charge is a young woman with little walking experience. The man used his mobile to call for help.'

'Why doesn't the mountain rescue team get up there?'

Josh's voice was grim. 'They can only be in one place at one time, and they've already been called out to two incidents. That school party could use a doctor so I'm going. Two doctors would be even better.'

She felt sick. 'Striding Edge was where I fell. Josh, I just couldn't.' She closed her eyes, had the vision again of tumbling through rocks, of pain and eventual blackness. He didn't speak and she cried, 'You don't know what you're asking me!'

He smiled bleakly. 'Of course not. I'm sorry. Don't worry, I can cope very well on my own.'

They were now in Glenridding and he drove to the beginning of the path up the mountain. Rain drummed on the car roof more heavily than ever. It wasn't a good day to walk in.

She turned and looked as Josh ran to the boot of the car, changed into his boots and put on the rest of his heavy weather gear. Then he loaded his doctor's equipment into a rucksack. His doctor's bag—of course. He frowned and took morphine from the box of medicines—he might need to administer pain relief. Then there were extra dressings, bandages, elastic supports. Other supplies from the emergency case. When he had finished, the rucksack looked heavy.

He came to the front of the car, leaned in and kissed her briefly. 'No need for you to wait here. Drive down into the village and have a cup of tea or something. I'll find you when I get back.' Then she watched him stride off into the swirling rain.

Have a cup of tea or something. She was needed, both

as a doctor and a lover, and she had been sent to have a cup of tea or something. She wept, tears of sadness, loss, fear and shame.

The rucksack was heavy and the uphill path now a stream bed. Mud clung to Josh's boots, making walking hard and treacherous. He tried to maintain a steady pace, knowing it was foolish to move too fast and then have to stop. He was alone on the hillside.

He tried to think about where he was going, what he might find, but his thoughts kept returning to Erin. He knew she was wrong about them. Should he try harder to persuade her, to bully her even? He felt—he hoped—that he could make her happy. But he knew that if she accepted him reluctantly, all that would come of it would be misery for both of them. The decision had to come from her. But how he wished she'd have him!

He tramped on, hood up and head down, seeing only the wet path in front of him, hearing only the rattle of the rain.

After about half an hour he vaguely thought that there was a sound behind him. He knew that the mountain rescue team would be coming eventually—perhaps they had got free earlier. He turned to look.

No mountain rescue team, just one slim figure bundled up as he was. He recognised the figure and the stride through the mist. Already his heart was beating rapidly through the exertion. Now it gave a great bound. It was Erin.

He stopped and she quickly caught up with him. She was as fit as ever.

'My rucksack is empty,' she said. 'Give me some of the stuff you're carrying and we'll both move faster.'

'What are you doing here? You must be terrified.'

'You told me that two doctors would be better than
one. Now you've got two doctors.' She took the strap
of his rucksack, helped him off with it. He put some of
the medical kit in her empty bag.

'I'm still worried about you.'

'Don't bother. I'm terrified but I'll cope.'

He put his arms round her and kissed her. Her face
was wet like his and they felt clumsy in their sodden
clothing. But it was good to kiss her. 'You can do it,
Erin, but don't push yourself. I'll help you and—'

She pushed him forcibly away. 'Right now I don't
want your love and I don't want your understanding and
I don't want your help! I've got to face this on my own.'

He looked at her, saw the stray strands of wet blonde
hair across her face and thought that he had never loved
her as he did now. He wanted to tell her so much but...

'Just follow me,' he said. 'If I'm moving too quickly,
yell.' He set off, confident she was behind him.

The decision had been the hardest Erin had ever made.
But no matter how much the terror, she could not just
sit in the village and drink tea. But when she had pulled
on her own kit, tightened her bootlaces, slid on the
empty rucksack, pulled forward her hood—then it had
been hard.

The thought of what lay ahead, of going to the very
place where she had fallen—the horror had been so great
that she'd hardly been able to move. She had clutched
the side of the car, tears swelling behind tightly closed
lids. She couldn't do it!

But she would. She had let go the car, placed one foot
forward and moved. Then another step, then another
step, then another. After all, this was why she had come

to the Lake District, to conquer her fears. She hadn't fully succeeded yet.

It had got easier as she had moved—just a bit. After a while she had seen Josh's figure ahead of her. She had been moving faster because she was carrying no load. And the sight of him had brought her comfort. In time she had caught up with him.

There was little time for explanations. They were doctors and they were wanted. Together, they moved on.

In the rain and mist it wasn't too bad. She couldn't see the great cliffs, the heights around her. But she knew they were there, and her terror lurked just below the surface.

Eventually they reached the top of the first slope and came out onto a plateau. Ahead was Red Tarn and then the shadow that was Helvellyn. On her left somewhere was Striding Edge. Where she had fallen—and where now the children had fallen.

Josh stopped, consulted his map, compass and satellite navigator. Then, confidently, he walked forward. She knew he had a grid reference for the children. Thank heaven for that.

It happened occasionally. The wind blew the mist away, and there in awesome clarity was the dark, wet height of Striding Edge. It reared above Erin and her terror was so great that she bit her lip till it bled. She tried to move faster, tire herself, so her body's agony could still her mind's fear.

And then she heard a voice. 'Here, over here.' She saw an arm waving. They had found the group.

There were eleven of them huddled in the lee of a great rock, not a bad place to shelter. They had had the sense to stay together in one place. They looked wet and bedraggled, but all seemed adequately dressed—one good thing.

A girl of about twenty-one came towards them, relief evident on her face. 'Are you the mountain rescue? Only Mr Evans is only just hanging on and I don't know what to do. Where's the rest of you?'

Erin guessed that she was a new teacher, obviously worried and scared that she couldn't cope. She made Erin feel older and even confident.

Josh said, 'The mountain rescue team is on its way. We're both doctors. We'll take charge here now. Who're you and who's this Mr Evans?'

'I'm Marie Morgan. Mr Evans is the PE teacher. His leg is broken and his head's bleeding. He managed to crawl under that rock but he says he's still in charge and we do what he says.'

'Anyone else badly hurt?'

'Well, we all skidded down and fell over a bit. There's bruises and scratches and I think there's a sprained ankle and perhaps a broken finger. I've done what I can with the first-aid box.'

'You look at this Mr Evans,' Erin suggested to Josh, 'and I'll do triage on the rest. We might be luckier than we thought.'

Josh nodded. 'Good idea.'

It was hard, trying to conduct examinations when the rain was sheeting down and she couldn't really remove much clothing. But there was a little shelter and she managed. Erin asked everyone how they had fallen, were there any pains, any lack of movement. She felt one boy's ribs—bruised but nothing broken there. Another had a nasty gash on his upper arm—she told him to keep pressing the dressing to it. A girl had wrenched her knee, but she could walk on it—slowly. And as Marie had said, there was a broken finger and a sprained ankle. Nothing life-threatening. And since they were reasonably dressed there was little danger of hypothermia.

She went to kneel by Josh, who was bending over a man lying flat in the shelter of a rock. This man was badly injured. His leg was distorted and blood was leaking from a dressing pressed to his forehead. Josh was drawing up morphine as the pain on the man's face was obvious.

'Mr Evans, Dr Hunter,' Josh said.

'Glad you got here,' the man muttered. 'Had to stay awake because these are my charges. Marie is all right but she's not trained…'

'You've both done very well,' Josh said. 'This could have been a tragedy, because of you it isn't. Now, I'm going to give you an injection for the pain, then you can sleep a bit. And I'll see to your leg and your head.'

'See to the pupils first!'

'Your pupils are in pretty good shape,' Erin said, 'and I'm seeing to them.'

Seconds later Mr Evans was asleep.

'He's lost a lot of blood,' Josh said. 'I'm going to fit him with a giving set. He needs the plasma expander. But we can't move him, we'll have to wait for the heavy team with the proper stretcher. How are the kids?'

'Not too bad. They're wet, lost and miserable, but so far they aren't too cold.'

'Can they walk?'

'One sprained ankle, one wrenched knee. They can walk if I put an elastic bandage on each, but they won't move very fast.'

'I want you to lead them down to the village while I stay here with Mr Evans till help comes.'

'Me lead them down! I only managed to get here be-cause I had you to lean on.'

'You did not. You did it yourself. Now take the next step. Make sure all these children are fit to move then take them down to the village. Can you use a compass and map?'

'Of course I can!'

'Then there's no problem. You're a doctor, you're do-ing what's best for your patients. Your own feelings don't matter.'

'That's easy for you to say.'

But she did as he suggested. She marshalled her group into a line, put Marie at the end and told her that no one was to lag behind her. There was a whistle if Marie wanted the line to stop. She put stronger boys beside the girl with the wrenched knee and the boy with the sprained ankle and told them to help. Then, slowly, they set off.

They managed. Progress was slow but there wasn't much grumbling—at least they were doing something now. Erin had to navigate by compass for the first half-hour, carefully walking round the rocks and small scree runs that littered the ground. But then they reached the top of the path into the valley and things were easier.

They moved slowly downwards. Erin put a steady-looking girl at the head of the line and moved up and down it, checking on everyone's progress and feelings. They were doing well.

And suddenly something happened to her.

She found she wasn't afraid any more. She was a competent doctor and an experienced walker, doing a good job in terrible conditions. And she was enjoy-ing it!

She couldn't help it. She lifted both arms over her head to the wet skies and screamed, 'Yes!'

'You all right, miss?' a slightly alarmed lad asked.

'Never been better,' she told him.

CHAPTER NINE

TEN minutes later figures loomed out of the mist ahead of them—six burly men carrying all sorts of kit and moving fast. 'Are you St Paul's School?' the leader asked. 'We're the mountain rescue team.'

Decisions were made quickly. Four men went on to carry Mr Evans down and two men stayed with Erin to escort the party down. 'We've got a stretcher,' one man said. 'Is there anyone who really shouldn't be walking, Doctor?'

Her professional opinion was being asked. 'You could carry the boy with the sprained ankle, then we'd all move a bit faster.'

It was anticlimactic when they got down to the village. A bus was waiting to take away the children. They would be kept warm, fed and given dry clothes, checked over in hospital. If necessary, they would be admitted. She was asked if she wanted to come, too, but she declined. She gave a quick report on what she had done and then the bus pulled away.

'Going to see you up a mountain again soon, Doctor?' one of the mountain rescue team asked. 'You were doing well up there.'

'Yes, you might see me some time.'

Then the two men walked back up to meet their mates and she was left alone.

Of all things, she walked down into the village and did as Josh had suggested—she had some tea. She took his flask and had it refilled. Then she went back and sat in the car to wait for him.

It was a couple of hours before the team arrived, carrying Mr Evans. An ambulance had arrived shortly before that and had waited, its engine running. The injured man was slid into the ambulance and it drove away. There were a few last words, some handshakes and then the rescue team were gone, too. Josh came over to her.

Erin got out of the car and hugged him, soaking wet though he was. 'Are you OK?' he asked.

'Couldn't be better, never felt better.'

He eased her away from him so he could look into her eyes, but held onto her arms. 'You mean that, don't you? You really do feel good. What's happened to you?'

'I don't know. But it's the most wonderful thing that happened to me in the past two years.' She thought for a moment and then said, 'Well, the second most wonderful thing.'

'I see.' He pushed his hood back and she saw that glorious curly hair, now damp and bedraggled. Well, her hair was probably just as bad. 'Look, I just don't believe it!'

They turned and looked together. The rain had stopped, the mist was rolling away. There was even the suggestion of sunshine. 'The Lake District,' he said. 'If you don't like the weather, just wait five minutes.'

'I think I've had enough of Helvellyn for a while,' she said. 'But we will come back.' She pointed across the lake. 'There's a good walk along the ridge at Angletarn Pikes. How about next weekend?'

'Already looking forward to it.' He studied her uncertainly. 'Am I missing something here?'

'Not if I can help it.' She glanced at her watch. 'It's only four o'clock. As I remember, we were having a conversation when this mountain got in our way. I refuse to continue it when I'm wet through. It'll only take an hour to get home—let's go back. We'll have a bath, change and have a drink, then talk in the warmth of the cottage.'

'How about a talk in the warmth of a bed?' he asked.

They reported to Cal where they were and what they had done, then they drove back to their cottages.

'We go to my house,' she said. 'I nearly lost you—I nearly let you go, that is. I'm not going to do the same again. I'm going to have the first bath because I've got to dry my hair afterwards and it takes ages. But I want you in there with me and you can wash my back and then have your own bath.'

'Isn't there room in there for the two of us together?'

'A lovely idea, but no. You know how small the bath is.'

Making sure no one could see, they stripped off their sodden clothes in the kitchen, they could put them in the washing machine later. Then they went upstairs and Josh washed Erin's back as she soaked there. His hands were warm and comforting, and as they slid over her she closed her eyes with pleasure. 'Not yet,' she said. 'But soon.' She didn't want to get out, it felt so good. But she knew there was more, and better, to come. Eventually he helped her to stand and step out. And as she dried her hair he bathed, too. Then together they went to bed.

'The sun's out now,' she said, 'but it's evening and there's no rays shining through my crystal.'

'There will be in the morning,' he said. 'We can watch them dance across the ceiling. If I'm still here in bed with you, that is.'

'You'd better be.'

He put his arm round her and kissed her. A gentle kiss, there was no hurry now she knew that there was all the time in the world.

'Am I mistaken,' he asked, 'or did some kind of miracle happen on that mountain?'

'You're not mistaken. I'm cured, and you cured me.'

Josh shook his head. 'Whatever happened, you managed it yourself. I left you behind—not happily perhaps, but I left you. You were the one who chose to follow me.' He looked at the ceiling, frowning. 'You said you didn't want my love, my understanding or my help, that it was something you had to do on your own.'

'Did I say that? Josh, I'm sorry!'

'Don't be sorry. I don't think I've ever loved you more than I did then. That was the old Erin talking and I was glad to see her back.'

'I feel so good,' she said. 'I feel happy and confident. I don't hate mountains any more and I know I can get on with people. Josh, I've laid my ghosts!'

'You're the Golden Girl again,' he said. He ran his fingers through the tresses that ran over her shoulders, down to her breasts. Then he eased aside the sheet to survey her nakedness. 'Golden all over.'

Primly, she pulled the sheet back. 'Josh! You're not supposed to make comments like that.' Then she threw the sheet aside. 'Yes, you can! I don't care any more.'

'Now you've uncovered me as well,' he pointed out.

'And how,' she said, and this time Josh blushed.

'It's like I was a train that had stopped in a tunnel,' she said. 'Everything was dark and there was no hope of ever getting out. But now I am out, and the sun is shining and I can hardly remember what the dark was like. Josh, I'm so happy!'

'Sweetheart, so am I.' He smiled lazily. 'Of course, there's a lot still to do. We've got the rest of the year to learn how to be good GPs. We haven't known each other that long, there's a lot of time to get to know each other better.'

'That's fine,' she said. 'I'm getting to know all of you ever so much better and I'd like to…'

Firmly, he removed her hand. 'In a minute,' he said. 'When I'm qualified I'd like to stay round here. But there's two of us to make decisions and you've got this flat in London which—'

'I'll sell it,' she said, 'and I let Jeremy know that I'm not going to go to America. I like it here, too. Now, is the serious conversation over?'

'Over,' he agreed. 'Now we can…'

EPILOGUE

JOSH was home first, so when Erin finally came in there was supper cooking in the oven.

It was four months since—well, since, and they still technically occupied two cottages. All this meant was that they alternated between the two. They had told Cal that as soon as he needed a free cottage they would share one.

Josh must have heard her crunching up the lane because before she had chance to open the door he had opened it for her. 'What a gorgeous night,' he said. Together, they looked upwards.

Two days ago the sky had been almost black with cloud, yesterday the first few flakes had wandered down and now there was a foot of snow outside. But the sky had cleared, there were bright stars in the darkness of the sky and the clean crescent of a new moon. 'Gorgeous,' she agreed.

She stepped inside and he closed the door behind her. Then she kicked off her boots, pulled off her woollen hat and scarf and was starting to unbutton her coat.

Josh smiled and bent to kiss her. 'You've got a cold nose,' he said.

'I've got cold everything. Josh, don't put your arms round me, you'll only get wet and I... Oh, all right. We can warm up together in front of the fire.'

'I'm warm enough for both of us,' he said.

Minutes later she was lying with her back to him on the couch, his arms around her waist and her feet outstretched to the flames of the wood fire. She wriggled comfortably. 'I've just been to see Lyn's new baby,' she said. 'He's lovely, perfect. A little boy with a mat of brown hair and rosebud lips.'

Josh squeezed her. 'So what does a midwife think of actually having a baby?'

Erin giggled. 'She said that she's been giving advice on having babies for years. She thought she was a good midwife. And she's just realised that she didn't know what she was talking about. Josh, she's over the moon!'

'I bet. Was Adam there?'

'He certainly was. He was as happy as she was. Josh, I've never seen a family so happy. Lyn was crying with joy.'

Josh kissed the top of her head. 'Something to think about,' he said. 'Anyone else visiting? I've arranged to call in myself tomorrow afternoon.'

'Lyn'll be so pleased to see you. She wants to show off her new baby. And, yes, Cal and Jane were there. And since we're all medical people, they bent the rules a little, and Helen was there, too. She's changed her mind now. She doesn't want to be a doctor, she wants to be a midwife.'

'Probably a wise choice. Now, let me guess. Did she point out that her pink bridesmaid's dress still fitted her, and that it would be entirely suitable for christenings as well as weddings?'

'I think the pink dress did come up in the conversation.' Erin reached behind her and pulled Josh's head down so she could kiss him. The she giggled again. 'Josh, remember Cal telling us that in diagnosis what people don't say is often as important as what they do say?'

'I remember that. Very true, too.'

'Well, Jane didn't say anything much. But she kept looking at the baby, then at Cal, then around the room, then at Helen and then at the baby again.'

'Just a district nurse, being professional, making sure that everything was all right?' Josh suggested with a grin.

'Not that at all. It was the look of a woman who is either pregnant now or expecting and intending to get that way in the next few weeks.'

'I see. Now that shows super-diagnostic skills. Who needs ultrasound? And what can you tell me about Cal?'

'Cal felt exactly the same way. Of course, he was very happy for Lyn and Adam, but his mind was on other things, too.'

'Fair enough. They've been married for three months now.'

'Yes,' said, Erin, 'and that wedding was something else.'

Recently there had been two weddings in the practice. Lyn had been married before and she had told Adam that she didn't want a big ceremony. Besides, she was decidedly pregnant. So they had married quietly, with just a couple of dozen close friends and colleagues from the practice.

Jane's and Cal's wedding had been different. There had been a church service with a full choir, a reception in a nearby hotel and dancing till the small hours. It had been a memorable night.

For Erin, however, there had been one more than magic moment, something that she remembered and promised herself that she would have, too. Usually, in the wedding service, the marrying couple followed the vicar's lead, repeating after him, 'I, Calvin, take thee, Jane…' But on this occasion Cal and Jane had memorised the words, turning to face each other and speaking without any prompting. It had been very moving.

Josh had taken her left hand and was kissing it. He often did this, a small, loving caress that made Erin feel needed and cherished.

'You know I've spoken to Cal about a junior partnership here,' he said after a while. 'The practice is going to expand, there are new plans for a local cottage hospital and my training period will be over before we know it.'

'I know,' she said. 'And I want you to stay here. And I want to stay here with you.'

He kissed the tip of her little finger. 'When we decided we were serious about each other, we decided to give ourselves some time. A few months to get to know each other.'

'So we did. And I have to say that you're not exactly what I thought you'd be.'

'I'm not?'

'No. You're even better.' She settled herself more comfortably against him, made sure he was still kissing her hand. 'You can do that again if you like.'

From the kitchen was coming the most appetising of smells, but she didn't want to move yet. She was too comfortable. It was good to lie here in the warmth and have her hand kissed.

When he spoke next his voice was tentative. 'You were a bit unsure of yourself when you first came here,' he said. 'You told me you'd come to lay ghosts.'

'I did and I have. I've got you now and you're no ghost.' She rubbed against him gently and said, 'I can tell.'

'You didn't know whether you were engaged or not. There was a ring that you didn't want.'

'And now I gather you've given it back to David. Good. He can sell it and buy another one for Cassie, they're getting engaged. D'you think they'll be as happy as us, Josh?'

'No. But I don't begrudge them what happiness they have.'

He moved against her, leaned over backwards to pick something up. 'New moon tonight, Erin. You wish on a new moon. And I've got a wish.'

Now he was kissing another fingertip. The one next to her little finger.

'What wish?' she asked hoarsely.

From somewhere there appeared a ring. It slid onto her finger and she gazed at the glitter of gold, the blaze of small diamonds, the cool beauty of a central emerald.

'My wish is to get engaged to you,' he said. 'Will you marry me, Erin?'

She could have waited before answering but there was no point. 'Of course I will,' she said.

Modern Romance™
...seduction and
passion guaranteed

Tender Romance™
...love affairs that
last a lifetime

Medical Romance™
...medical drama
on the pulse

Historical Romance™
...rich, vivid and
passionate

Sensual Romance™
...sassy, sexy and
seductive

Blaze Romance™
...the temperature's
rising

27 new titles every month.

Live the emotion

MILLS & BOON®

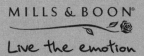

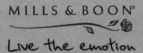

MILLS & BOON

STEPHANIE LAURENS

A Season for Marriage

Available from 18th July 2003

*Available at most branches of WH Smith,
Tesco, Martins, Borders, Eason, Sainsbury's
and all good paperback bookshops.*

0703/135/MB67

4 FREE

books and a surprise gift!

We would like to take this opportunity to thank you for reading this Mills & Boon® book by offering you the chance to take FOUR more specially selected titles from the Medical Romance™ series absolutely FREE! We're also making this offer to introduce you to the benefits of the Reader Service™—

- ★ FREE home delivery
- ★ FREE gifts and competitions
- ★ FREE monthly Newsletter
- ★ Exclusive Reader Service discount
- ★ Books available before they're in the shops

Accepting these FREE books and gift places you under no obligation to buy, you may cancel at any time, even after receiving your free shipment. Simply complete your details below and return the entire page to the address below. *You don't even need a stamp!*

YES! Please send me 4 free Medical Romance books and a surprise gift. I understand that unless you hear from me, I will receive 6 superb new titles every month for just £2.60 each, postage and packing free. I am under no obligation to purchase any books and may cancel my subscription at any time. The free books and gift will be mine to keep in any case.

M3ZEE

Ms/Mrs/Miss/Mr ....Initials......................................
BLOCK CAPITALS PLEASE

Surname ....

Address ....

....

....Postcode..............................

Send this whole page to:
UK: FREEPOST CN81, Croydon, CR9 3WZ
EIRE: PO Box 4546, Kilcock, County Kildare (stamp required)